"Okay, here are the Rules of Pretend Dating Lexie," she said. "You need to *stop* comparing me to a giant gorilla."

"What are the other rules?" Jake asked.

"That's the only one," she said. Was her voice shaking? Could he tell? "So far. I'll keep you posted as others come up." She looked back from the doorway. "Coming, Jake?"

"You bet," he said, standing up and stretching. "Where my girlfriend goes, I go."

Lexie shivered.

I always thought my first boyfriend would be Jake. But I never thought it would only be pretend . . .

i ❤ bikinis

He's With Me by Tamara Summers

Island Summer by Jeanine Le Ny

What's Hot by Caitlyn Davis

i ♥ bikinis

He's With Me

Tamara Summers

Point

For Dayna, with love and pugs—TTS

No part of this work may be reproduced, stored in a retrieval
system, or transmitted in any form or by any means, electronic,
mechanical, photocopying, recording, or otherwise, without
written permission of the publisher. For information regarding
permission, write to Scholastic Inc., Attention: Permissions
Department, 557 Broadway, New York, NY 10012.

ISBN-13: 978-0-439-91850-3
ISBN-10: 0-439-91850-2

Copyright © 2007 by Tui Sutherland

SCHOLASTIC, POINT, and associated logos are trademarks
and/or registered trademarks of Scholastic Inc.

12 11 10 9 8 7 6 5 4 3 2 1   7 8 9 10 11 12/0
01

Printed in the U.S.A.
First printing, May 2007

He's With Me

chapter 1

Lexie Willis hated bikinis.

At fifteen, she already had too many curves in too many places, and she didn't like people staring at her. Putting on a bikini made her feel like Janet Jackson at the Super Bowl even when she was just standing alone in a Macy's dressing room.

So *why* was there a bikini in the box on her bed?

The box *looked* like a present. It had shiny gold foil wrapping paper and a cheerful bright green bow, as if to trick her into thinking, *Hey, there's something* fun! *and* exciting! *in here!* There was even a little card on top that read: FOR LEXIE! IT'S GOING TO BE A GREAT SUMMER! in her mother's perky, exclamation-point-happy handwriting.

But inside the box was this wine-red monstrosity. Lexie didn't even pull it out all the way before she realized what it was and stuffed the pieces

1

back in, hiding them under the folds of white tissue paper.

Seriously, Mom? Seriously?

The other box was even more mysterious. She could tell from its large, long, flat shape that it wasn't a book or an Amazon gift certificate, which was disappointing right up front. But she was hoping for a new sundress, perhaps — maybe one she could wear *over* the bikini. And never take off.

Instead, it was a tennis racket.

Lexie didn't play tennis. She had never played tennis in her life.

This was very ominous.

Lexie was standing next to her bed, examining the tennis racket, when her mother appeared in the doorway.

"Isn't it *great*?" Mrs. Willis said happily. "I made sure your father got the best one. Is it light enough for you?"

"Um," Lexie said. Her twin brother, Colin, followed Mrs. Willis into the room and slouched against the door frame. He didn't look any happier than she was. Maybe he'd gotten some sinister, inappropriate presents, too.

Lexie's mom sat down on the bed and pulled

the bikini out of the box, laying it out flat on the comforter. It wasn't as bad as Lexie had thought — not as skimpy as the little white bikinis Bree McKennis always wore, for instance. And it was her favorite color. But still. There was no way she was wearing that.

"Colin, are you as confused as I am?" Lexie asked. "Does Mom think the Holy Spirit of Athletic Daughters Everywhere has finally arrived to possess me?"

Colin shrugged, and Lexie's mom batted at her with the top of the bikini box. "I'm right here, Lexie," her mom said. "You can ask *me* these questions, you know." Of course, she didn't wait for Lexie to ask. "It's for Summerlodge."

"The day camp?" Lexie said. "I thought Colin and I were doing the art program at the school. Mom, did you get paintbrushes and tennis rackets mixed up?"

"Turns out the art program was full," Lexie's mom said. "So you're doing Tennis for Teens instead. Won't that be fun? And Summerlodge is close enough for you to bike to, so that'll make it easier on me and your dad, too."

"Oh, *no*," Lexie said. "Mom, I *hate* tennis."

"You don't know that you hate tennis, dear,"

Mrs. Willis said. "You've never tried it. And this is what comes of waiting until too late to make your summer plans."

"Then what's *that* for?" Lexie asked, pointing at the bikini. "I hope I don't have to play tennis in *that*."

"There's a pool at Summerlodge," Mrs. Willis said. "One of the afternoon activities, after tennis practice, is swimming, which I thought you would like. Don't you like swimming?"

I do like swimming, Lexie thought. *I'd just prefer to do it fully clothed, thanks very much.*

"Lucky you already know how to play tennis," she said to Colin. Tennis had been one of Colin's brief obsessions, so he'd taken lessons long enough to be a decent player. "At least you'll definitely look cooler than me with one of these." She tried to flip the racket in one hand and dropped it on the floor.

Mrs. Willis sighed. "Well, that's the bad news. Colin's not going with you."

"What?" Lexie was horrified. The whole point of having a twin was that you never had to go anywhere by yourself. So you never had to stand around awkwardly, feeling like the pigeon in a flock of flamingos, while nobody talked to you.

4

You always had someone to stand awkwardly *with* you. That was the *whole point.* Colin still wouldn't meet her eyes. "But why? We were going to do it together!"

"We've decided Summerlodge is not what Colin needs right now," Lexie's mom said.

"Mom, that's not fair! Why does he get to stay home and play video games while I have to go out and look like an idiot all by myself?"

"It'll be good for you," Lexie's mom said firmly. "And look on the bright side: You might actually make some friends besides your brother." She stood up in a "conversation over" kind of way.

Lexie used to have a friend besides Colin: Karina Martinez, her best friend through all of elementary school. But Karina had moved to China a year before, and Lexie hadn't found anyone else. It was hard to make new friends at her school, where she would always be known as "Karina's quiet friend" or "quirky Colin's twin sister." And she was sure it wouldn't be any easier at summer camp all on her own.

"No, I won't!" Lexie cried. "Oh, Mom, I'll be the only person I know there! No one will talk to me and it'll be *so* awful; *please* don't make me go without Colin."

5

"You'll know someone else," Colin said, finally chiming in. "Jake's going to Summerlodge, too."

Thump-thump. Lexie felt her heart jump up and bang into her rib cage. Okay, that did make a difference.

Jake Atkinson was Colin's best friend, although they weren't very much alike. Colin was a quiet guy who got obsessed with funny things like stamp-collecting and bird-watching and, lately, filmmaking. Jake, on the other hand, was outgoing, adorable, smart, and funny, and as far as Lexie could tell, every freshman and sophomore girl at Carlisle High wanted to date him.

But Lexie's crush on Jake was different from everyone else's. It *was.* Those other girls liked him the way you like a movie star, but Lexie liked the real him. She knew why Jake was friends with Colin. She was there the day they met.

Back then, Jake was the new guy in town. He showed up for the first day of eighth grade and practically made girls swoon all the way down the hall. In Pre-Algebra, second period, Mr. Stone split Colin and Lexie up and sat Jake right in between them.

Lexie kept looking over at Colin, thinking of

things she wanted to tell him, but figuring it was too risky to pass a note through a stranger. The third time she looked over, hoping he'd noticed that Mr. Stone's bald spot was shaped exactly like a pineapple, she saw him watching Jake's hands. Jake was folding a piece of paper, over and over, and twisting it around. The twins both stared at him until suddenly, sitting on Jake's desk, there was a small origami whale that could fit in the palm of your hand.

With a studious expression, Jake drew eyes and a smiley face on the whale. Then he looked up and caught Lexie smiling at it. She looked away quickly, embarrassed.

When she glanced down again, the whale was sitting on the corner of her desk, beaming at her.

After class, as she was gathering her books, Colin leaned over to Jake.

"Hey," he said, "that was cool. It's origami, right? Can you make other stuff, too?" Lexie knew that Colin must be really interested, because he hardly ever talked to strangers. But once he started talking, it was pretty hard to make him stop.

"A few other things," Jake said. "My dad taught me. I can show you, if you want."

"Sure!" Colin said. "How about Saturday? You could come over for lunch."

"Don't you want to know my name before inviting me over?" Jake said with a cute smile.

"That dork is Colin," Lexie said. "My brother. I'm Lexie."

"Short for Alexandra," Colin said. "Like Alexander the Great. Or Alexander Helios, son of Cleopatra. Did you know Cleopatra had twins? A boy and a girl, like us. Alexander Helios and Cleopatra Selene." Colin's only lasting obsession was with random twin facts. He could list a ton of famous twins.

"I did not know that. I'm Jake," the new kid said, shaking Colin's hand solemnly. "Will you be there on Saturday?" he said to Lexie.

"Probably," she said. *Meaning definitely, if there's a chance you'll be there.* She knew Karina would be more than happy to come over and meet the cute new guy.

"Okay. Saturday would be great. Thanks, Colin."

The next day, Lexie saw Jake carrying around a library book about Cleopatra. He was the only guy she knew who read books for fun. But what he read was random nonfiction about things that caught his interest, like the Salem witchcraft trials or Aztec mythology or the life of Harry Houdini.

That was why he got along so well with Colin. Jake could probably have ditched them for a more popular crowd if he'd joined a sports team or auditioned for theater, but he liked Colin's strange interests. Whenever Colin found a new hobby, Jake read up on it. And then Lexie and Karina hung out with them while Colin built a replica of the HMS *Bounty* from a model shipbuilding kit and Jake told them strange facts about the famous mutiny.

So she knew the real Jake, just like she knew the real Colin, when nobody else did. Lexie thought of her front door as an enchanted mirror, like the looking glass Alice climbed through in the book. When she and Jake and Colin walked through it, they became their real selves. Here Colin talked as much as he wanted to. Here Jake thought she was funny.

Here she could imagine that maybe one day Jake would look at her and see Lexie, girl of his dreams, instead of Lexie, his best friend's sister.

She still had the whale. It was hidden in a shoe box in her room, next to other secret Jake things.

And nobody knew how she felt, not even Colin, who knew every single other detail of her life and every thought that ever crossed her mind.

"Jake?" Lexie said, picking up the tennis racket and trying to flip it again. She hoped the nervous shake in her voice would be hidden by the clatter of the falling racket. "He's going to tennis camp?"

Colin nodded. "He'll be in the advanced class, of course."

"Of course," Lexie said, losing hope again. Jake was one of the best tennis players in the school. And she was sure to be terrible, which probably wasn't the best way to impress him.

"Why can't *you* come with me?" Lexie said plaintively.

"Because I said so," Mrs. Willis interjected. "Remember me? Still in the room?"

"Moooooooooom," Lexie said, flopping onto her mattress and trying to look as woebegone as possible.

"It's all decided," Mrs. Willis said. "Camp starts tomorrow." She smoothed the bikini on the comforter again with a pleased expression. Lexie wished *she* would just take the darn bikini and wear it herself if she was so excited about it. If Lexie had to go swimming — in front of Jake, no less — she would be wearing the same simple black one-piece that she'd had for two years.

The doorbell rang. *Be booop bee booop . . . bee booop beeeee booooooop.* Lexie liked the weird chimes it played. Besides, it was the sound that usually meant Jake was there.

"That's Jake," Colin said. "He called and said he has some major problem and needs our advice. Although why he'd want to ask a moron like me is the real question."

"Oh, Colin," Mrs. Willis said. "Don't talk about yourself like that."

"It's probably another girl crisis," Lexie said. Jake was always having girl crises — either someone wanted to date him, or there was someone he wanted to date, or his current girlfriend was acting weird because he wasn't the 100 percent perfect boyfriend that she'd been expecting.

"I'll be down in a minute," Lexie called as Colin thumped down the stairs. She sat up and saw that her mom was still hovering.

"Don't you want to try it on?" Mrs. Willis said, gesturing at the bathing suit.

"Um," Lexie said. *With Jake in the house? I'd rather eat lizards.* "Maybe later." *Like in my next life, when I come back as a ditzy supermodel.*

11

"All right," Lexie's mom said with another sigh, and finally left the room.

Lexie ran over to the mirror and put on the necklace Jake had given her for her birthday the past November. She always wore it around him, for good luck. It was just a strand of small red glass beads, but she liked it.

She brushed her hair — dark brown, down to her shoulder blades, and way too fluffy — and scrunched her nose at the reflection. Well. She looked pretty much the same as she did every day, so if it hadn't worked yet, it probably wouldn't now.

Lexie found Colin and Jake, as usual, in the basement. Colin was playing with the zoom on the secondhand video camera he'd borrowed from Dad. Jake was still standing by the door, and when Lexie walked in, he threw open his arms and went, "Lexie!" in this big dramatic excited voice.

This was their new joke. The week before, Colin had asked them to act out a scene for his camera, and when Jake started doing everything all over-the-top and melodramatic, Lexie had followed along. They thought this was the most hilarious thing ever, and they couldn't get through three lines without falling over laughing. Colin didn't think it was quite so funny.

"Jake!" she cried now with the same dramatic enthusiasm.

"Oh, shut up," said Colin.

Jake held up his hand and Lexie high-fived him. As he walked back to the couch, she curled her fingers over her palm, holding in the warm, tingly feeling his hand had left behind.

"So what's the new crisis, Jake?" Colin said, setting the camera on the coffee table and kneeling to peer through it. He never seemed all that interested in Jake's girl problems, but Lexie thought it made Colin feel better to hear that even if you could get a girlfriend, it wasn't always easy after that. He still hadn't dated anyone, and as far as she knew, he'd never liked anyone, either. At least she'd dated Dave Mitchell for a week in seventh grade, if you could call holding hands and awkwardly slow-dancing at one party "dating."

"It's the end of the world," Jake said as Lexie sat down on the other end of the couch from him. "I'm totally doomed. Hey, Lexie, did you know that Ewan McGregor, Brad Pitt, and Will Smith were all offered the role of Neo in *The Matrix* before Keanu Reeves got it? They turned it down. Isn't that crazy?"

"It would have been much funnier with Will Smith," she said. Some days Jake's eyes were really blue, but today he was wearing a mossy-green T-shirt that made them look a cool stormy gray color.

"Colin, you should make a movie like *The Matrix*," Jake said. "Lexie could play Trinity."

"No problem," Colin said. "I was wondering what to do with that two hundred million dollars just lying around in my bank account."

"Oh, but," Lexie said, snapping her fingers, "I'm afraid my leather catsuit is in the laundry. Too bad."

"That *is* too bad," Jake said earnestly. "I had this whole series of you-in-black-leather movies planned. *X-Men, Catwoman, King Kong* . . . I'd be Naomi Watts and you'd be Kong, of course."

"Shut *up*," Lexie said, flinging a throw pillow at him.

"What?" he said with a grin. "It's the grandest love story ever told."

Luckily Colin interrupted before Lexie had to respond to *that*.

"Hello?" said her brother. "Crisis? Aren't we here for a reason? You don't sound all that doomed."

"I am," Jake said. "I'm totally doomed."

"Why?" Lexie asked. As far as she knew, Jake had been single for a couple of months, ever since Amy Sorrento had broken up with him for not calling her every single day. So it was probably a girl-he-wanted-to-date category of problem.

"Bree McKennis," said Jake.

Lexie's heart sank. Bree was the classic popular girl — blond, beautiful, and blissfully mean. Once she got her hooks into someone, they stayed hooked, even after she dumped him. If Jake had fallen for someone like her, Lexie didn't stand a chance. In fact, if Jake had fallen for someone like her, maybe Lexie didn't know him that well after all.

"Bree McKennis?" Colin said. "She's . . . isn't she kind of out of your league? She's, like, *really* popular."

"Sadly, apparently not," Jake said. "She wants to go out with me. Maybe she sees some untapped popularity potential in me. If so, I vote for not tapping it. It can stay right where it is, thanks."

"*Bree* wants to go out with *you*?" Colin said.

Lexie was relieved, but she did not appreciate

Colin's shocked tone of voice. Why wouldn't anyone want to go out with Jake?

"Yup," Jake said. "She informed me of this in an e-mail."

"No way," Lexie said.

"See for yourself." Jake pulled a piece of paper out of his back jeans pocket, unfolded it, and slid it over to her.

Jakey,

Have you ever wondered what it would be like to date the hottest girl in school? I bet you have. I could tell you were thinking about it when I got lemonaid from you at my sister's graduation ceremony. You were thinking, "If only Bree would ever date me." Well, it's your lucky summer. I have decided that I need a boyfriend and here are the reasons we would be the perfect couple:

(1) our heights would match perfectly,

(2) we'll both be at Summerlodge this summer,

(3) we're both cute and popular,

(4) and so we'd be like the Angelina Jolie and Brad Pitt of Summerlodge, only without the smelly orphans.

I imagine this feels like winning the lottery, doesn't it? Not that I'd notice if I did, since I'm already so rich, but I'm guessing you would, and it would be like just as way exciting as this. I'll meet you tomorrow at the front gate of Summerlodge so we can make our entrance together. Then I'll also debreef you on the Rules of Dating Bree. How awesome will this be?

Kisses,
Bree

"Oh, *Jakey*," Lexie said, passing it on to Colin. "How can you resist?"

"I know," Jake said. "It's better than winning the lottery. It's like winning the lottery and falling down a well and being vomited on by a llama all at the same time."

Lexie laughed. "So she's going to be at Summerlodge, too? Does she play tennis?" *Lord, please don't let her be in the Beginners class with me. Please find some other horrible way of torturing me instead.*

"Nope, she's working at the pool — training to be a lifeguard. So hopefully we won't have to see her too much."

Colin flattened out the printed e-mail on the

table and videotaped it. "This is crazy," he said. "I didn't know girls ever did this kind of thing."

"Bree McKennis does anything she wants," Jake said. "Which is why you guys have to save me. I can't date her! First, it'll be painful and agonizing. She'll make me carry her things and bring her sodas and buy her stuff, and then she'll yell at me when I do anything wrong, and then she'll make fun of me to all her friends behind my back, and *then* she'll dump me and tell *everyone* what a dork I am and I'll never get a date in this town ever again. I may not be the world's most popular guy, but this will ruin me for the rest of high school. Remember what she did to Kevin Barkett? Or Alvaro? No, you don't, because once she was through with them, they disappeared from everyone's minds. *Forever*."

"However," said Colin, "she is really hot. Like, Angelina Jolie–type hot."

"Ew, Colin!" Lexie said, smacking his shoulder.

"She is!" Colin said. "Right, Jake?"

Jake shrugged. "I guess she's okay. Not my type."

"Not your — seriously?"

"Personally, I would've stayed with Jennifer Aniston," Jake said. "And did you miss the part about the 'Rules of Dating Bree'? Does that sound like fun to you? Man, I *knew* I shouldn't have met her eyes when she came up to get lemonade. I shouldn't have agreed to work the concessions stand at graduation in the first place. Now it's going to be the worst summer ever." He slid onto the floor, lay down, and crossed his arms over his face.

"Can't you just say no?" Colin asked.

"Even I know the answer to that," Lexie said. "Nobody says no to Bree." Lexie understood exactly what Jake was worried about. She'd been avoiding Bree since elementary school. If you stayed far under her radar, you could slip by unnoticed and unharmed, but if you popped into her line of sight in any way, she would rip you to shreds with one flick of her French-tipped nails.

"Doomed," Jake muttered. "Doooomed."

"All right," Colin said. "Tell her you already have a girlfriend."

Jake thought for a minute. "Like, long-distance? I don't think she'll buy that. Plus it's only been a week since school ended. Where would I have picked up a girlfriend in a week?"

"I dunno." Colin shrugged. "You could tell her you're dating Lexie."

Lexie was so, so, *so* glad that Colin had his eyes glued to the camera controls and didn't see her expression. Jake kept his arms over his face, so he didn't notice, either. She felt like she might faint. There was a really awkward pause, and Lexie wondered if she was supposed to make a joke here.

She started to say, "As if —" at the same time as Jake said, "Well, I —" and they both stopped.

"What were you going to say?" he asked. He put his arms down and tilted his head back to look at her.

"Um, just . . . as if she'll believe that."

"Why?" Colin said. Lexie wished Jake would say something, but he just kept looking at her.

"Well, if you think Bree is out of his league, then I'm in another solar system, aren't I?" she tried to joke.

"Actually, it might work," Jake said. Lexie bit her tongue, she was so surprised.

"Sure it will," Colin said. "Lexie will be at Summerlodge, too, so Bree can see you're together. And it's only for a little while, until Bree gets over you. And it's not like there's anyone Lexie wants to date, so you're hardly putting a dent in her love life. Right, Lexie?"

That's nice. Thanks, Colin.

"What do you say, Lexie?" Jake asked, rolling over onto his stomach and propping his elbows on the floor and his chin in his hands adorably. "Want to be my pretend girlfriend?" His eyes were like storm clouds, big and unstoppable and irresistible.

Lexie, this is what you've been dreaming about.

Correction: This is a strange parody of what you've been dreaming about. Is this really what you want? Being Jake's pretend girlfriend?

Yeah, sure, okay. Close enough!

"Okay," she said, feeling dizzy. "I mean, it'll be tough pretending to like you, but I guess I can take one for the team. Right?"

"You're my knight in shining armor," Jake said, getting up and kneeling on the couch next to her. *Right* next to her. "My hero, my warrior princess," he said, taking her hand. "My King Kong." He pressed her hand to his heart. She could actually feel it beating through the soft fabric of his shirt. It was going really fast. Nearly as fast as hers, but he was an athlete, so it probably went that fast all the time.

"Okay, here are the Rules of Pretend Dating Lexie," she said. "You need to *stop* comparing me to a giant gorilla."

"What are the other rules?" he asked. He was still holding her hand against his chest.

"That's the only one," she said. Was her voice shaking? Could he tell? "So far. I'll keep you posted as others come up."

He grinned. "I'll look forward to it."

"Okay," Colin said, standing up. "I think I've figured out how to change it to night recording. Let's go test it in the shed." He picked up a flashlight and headed for the stairs. Lexie couldn't believe her own twin hadn't noticed how much she was blushing. She wanted to stay where she was forever, but she pulled her hand free and scrambled off the couch.

"Great, okay," she said. "Sounds like fun." She looked back from the doorway. "Coming, Jake?"

"You bet," he said, standing up and stretching. "Where my girlfriend goes, I go."

Lexie shivered.

I always thought my first boyfriend would be Jake. But I never thought it would only be pretend....

♥ chapter 2

The next morning, Lexie was sitting on the front steps, tracing shapes in the dew with her sneaker, when Jake's bike appeared at the end of the block. She jumped up and checked for the tenth time whether her tennis racket was securely fastened to the back of her bike.

"Bye," Colin said from the doorway. One of their pugs, Thorn, pressed his face against the screen door next to him and made a sad noise. "Have fun."

"Yeah, right," she said. "*You're* the one who's going to have fun. I wish I could stay home all day, too."

He nodded, looking down at the ground. Mrs. Willis came up behind him and swung open the screen door. Thorn trotted out and nosed Lexie's ankle.

"Are you wearing enough sunscreen, Lexie?" her mother said anxiously. "Did you bring extra?

What about the hat; did you pack the hat I gave you?"

"Yes, Mom," Lexie said. "I'm wearing enough sunscreen to cover the entire population of Australia. I think I'll survive the sun; it's the pain and humiliation of tennis you should be worried about."

"Hey, Willis family," Jake said, skidding to a stop in the driveway. "Ready to go, Lexie?" She was glad he didn't make a girlfriend joke in front of her mom. That would have been tough to explain.

"Sure." She swung onto her bike. "Bye, Colin."

"Bye." He went back into the house. Mrs. Willis stayed on the porch, waving, until Lexie and Jake were halfway up the block and couldn't see her through the trees anymore.

Lexie had hardly been able to sleep all night. What was going to happen that day? What did being a pretend girlfriend mean? What would she have to do? Who would Jake tell? What would people think? She had no idea how to act around a real boyfriend, let alone a pretend one.

The wind whipped her hair back from her face as they coasted down the hill to the stop sign.

Lexie could feel Jake glancing over at her, and she wondered whether she looked like a sweaty mess already. As they paused at the corner, waiting for a car to pass, suddenly he leaned over and put one hand over hers on the handlebars. Lexie froze. She wanted him to leave it there, but she didn't want to seem obvious about wanting him to leave it there.

"Lexie," he said. She loved the way he said her name.

"Yeah?"

"Are you okay? You look nervous."

"Well," she said, "you know, tennis. Me and sports, a bad combination." *Wow, could I sound like a bigger dork?*

"You don't have to do this," he said. "If you don't want to. It's okay. I can find another way to get rid of Bree."

"Oh, that?" she said with a nervous laugh. "I'm not worried about that. Seriously. Um. It's the tennis. Nerve-wracking tennis." *Oh, and maybe the fact that I'm alone with Jake. No Colin. No Karina. Just me and Jake.*

"If you're sure," he said, taking his hand back to his own handlebars. Lexie took a deep breath.

"Besides, didn't you e-mail her already?" she

said. "We wouldn't want her to think I got sick of you that fast." She tried to smile.

"True," he said with a grin. "Okay, but just remember I really appreciate this." He lifted up and pedaled ahead, and it took her a minute to recover enough to follow him.

Summerlodge was down a winding road through pine trees. The camp had a pool, tennis and basketball courts, sports fields, and a large barn for indoor activities when it rained. A couple of different summer programs used the camp, but the one Lexie and Jake were doing was Tennis for Teens.

As they coasted into the parking lot, Lexie spotted a thin, tan figure in white shorts and a fitted white baby tee leaning against the big Summerlodge sign.

"Uh-oh," Jake muttered.

"I thought you told her," Lexie said. "Didn't you e-mail her?"

"I did," Jake said. "She didn't write back. Maybe she didn't get it."

Lexie felt an anvil of cold dread settle into her stomach. She'd spent so much time thinking about how to pretend to be Jake's girlfriend that she'd completely forgotten about what Bree

McKennis might do to her. Stealing Bree's chosen boyfriend — that definitely didn't qualify as staying under her radar.

"Just ignore her," Jake said.

"Very funny," said Lexie.

They got off their bikes and rolled them into the bike rack. As Lexie knelt to wrap her lock through the front wheel, she heard the clip-clop of Bree's high-heeled sandals coming closer, as if an elegant angel of death were approaching.

"Hi, Jake," Bree said in her sultry voice. Lexie had always thought Bree was too skinny to have a voice so low, but it made her sound like an old-time movie star. It also made her sound bored a lot of the time. That, or she really was that bored.

"Hey, Bree," Jake said. How did he sound so casual? "This is my girlfriend, Lexie."

Lexie's hands were shaking, so she could barely clip her lock into place, but she finally snapped it in and stood up. Bree McKennis was studying her with narrow blue eyes. Her hair was pale, shiny blond and perfectly straight, cut in a close bob so that a sharp wing of hair hung down on each side of her face. She kept pushing it back with one long, tan, manicured hand. Bree loved to wear white to show off her tan, and she always seemed to stay that color all year long. Colin was convinced that it was fake, and that she went to a salon or used some product. Whether that was true or not, Lexie's mom — World's Most Enthusiastic Supplier of Sunscreen — would have been appalled to see it.

"Lexie Willis," Bree said slowly. "I have seen you before." She narrowed her eyes even more. "I thought you moved away in elementary school."

Nope. I just got quieter and better at staying out of your way.

"Guess not," Jake said when Lexie didn't respond. "Lucky for me." He came around his bike and started helping Lexie unfasten her tennis racket from the back. Bree leaned against the bike rack, watching like a snake poised to strike. Lexie could barely breathe, she was so nervous. Could Bree tell that they were just pretending? What would she do if she figured it out?

Behind them, a car pulled up.

"Howdy-doo, Lexie!" a voice called, and Lexie winced. It was Mrs. Kim, her mother's friend. The Kims had moved to town a year before, and Mrs. Kim worked with Mrs. Willis at the library.

At first Lexie's mom had been convinced that Mrs. Kim's daughter Sally would be a perfect new best friend for Lexie after Karina left. But Sally was much too cool to hang out with Lexie. Bree had latched on to her from day one, so now Sally was one of the most popular girls in school.

Lexie waved at Mrs. Kim as Sally got out of the car and bounced over to the bike rack. Sally moved like there was always dance music playing in her head. She had perfect, really long, straight black hair, now back in a ponytail, and although she was short, like Lexie, she always looked long and graceful. She was wearing bright clean tennis whites, and Lexie glanced down at her scruffy khaki shorts and red T-shirt.

"Hey, Bree," Sally said as she came up.

"Sally," Bree said with a note of scandalized disapproval in her voice. "You're wearing white."

"Well, yeah," Sally said. "They're tennis whites. That's the idea."

"White is *my* color," Bree said.

Sally giggled. "Don't worry, Your Highness. My bathing suit is green. By the time I get to the pool, no one will ever know that I was so out of line."

Bree sniffed. "Sally, you remember Jake," she said meaningfully. "This is his *girlfriend*."

Sally squinted at Lexie. "No way. I didn't know you guys were dating."

Lexie suddenly had the horrible realization that if Sally knew, Mrs. Kim would know, and that meant Lexie's mom would hear the news before Lexie even had time to get home. But it was too late to do anything about that now.

"Um, yeah," Lexie said. "It's new."

"Really?" Bree said, rolling her *r*. "When did you guys get together?"

"Last Wednesday," Jake said.

"Friday," Lexie said at the same time.

Bree's eyebrows shot up.

"I asked her on Wednesday," Jake said quickly, "but she didn't say yes until Friday."

"Oh, how cute," Bree said in a tone that sounded more like "oh, how repulsive."

"How did he ask you?" Sally said. She sounded more interested than Bree. "Was it adorable? Or was it weird?"

Hmm, let's see. I think I'd have to go with weird.

"You know," Jake said, perhaps sensing Lexie's panic. "I just asked her. No big deal. We should go on in, shouldn't we?" He started forward and

Bree stopped him with one hand on his chest. Looking straight at Lexie, she draped herself over his shoulder.

"Oh, *boys*," she said in a teasing, aren't-we-all-friends-here way. "They never care about the details. To get the real story, you have to ask the girl. Right, Lexie? So tell us the details. I want to hear every single thing."

"It's totally boring," Jake said. "And we're going to be late."

"We have a few minutes," Bree said, resting her other hand on his arm so both hands were holding him in place. "Unless there's some reason you don't want her to tell this story, Jakey."

Jake and Lexie exchanged glances. Hers said, *She totally knows we're lying*. His said, *Help! What do we do?*

Lexie took a deep breath. Well, she had imagined Jake asking her out a thousand times. She could describe the perfect scene pretty easily.

"Um," she said. "It was Wednesday night. I decided to walk Thorn and Alanna — those are our dogs — to the park on the corner. When I came out the door, Jake was there, on the porch. He looked like he'd been waiting for a while, thinking about ringing the doorbell. I thought

31

that was weird, but he asked if he could come to the park, and I said sure. I gave him Alanna's leash because she doesn't tug on it as much as Thorn does."

"Your dogs are named Alanna and Thorn?" Sally interrupted. Bree glared at her, but she didn't notice. "Seriously?"

"It's from this series of books I like," Lexie said, blushing furiously. "Alanna and Thorn are twins, like me and Colin, so that's why we picked those names." She hadn't ever thought about her dogs' names being embarrassing before.

"Go on," Bree said. "So you and Jake walked up to the park."

"Yeah," Lexie said. "And we let the dogs off the leashes in the fenced area, and then we sat on this bench by the fountain."

"I know that fountain," Sally said. "Wow, that's so romantic."

"*Sally,*" Bree said. "Stop *interrupting.*"

"And then he put something in my hand," Lexie said. She had imagined it so many times, it was like it was real in her head. She could practically see the expression on his face in the moonlight. "I looked down, and it was this little origami whale. On one side it said, 'Lexie . . .' And when I turned it over, the other side said, '. . . will you be my girlfriend?'"

"Oh my *God*," Sally said. "That is the cutest thing I've *ever* heard."

"How could you read it in the moonlight?" Bree said suspiciously.

"There are, um, lights in the park," Lexie said, jolted back to reality. She glanced nervously at Jake, but she couldn't figure out the look on his face. Was he freaked out? Did he think it was weird that she had come up with that whole story off the top of her head?

"Oh," Bree said. "Well. That's sweet." She shoved Jake away from her. "I don't know why you didn't want to tell us *that* story, Jake."

"Guys don't like girls to know how romantic they can be," Lexie said, trying to sound like she had any idea what she was talking about.

"But you waited until Friday to say yes?" Bree asked. Lexie felt like she was being interrogated. The bright lights and water torture couldn't be far off.

"Um. I guess I was nervous," she said. "I haven't — I mean, Jake's my first —" She faltered. She couldn't do it. She couldn't say, "Jake's my boyfriend."

"The important thing is she did say yes," Jake said smoothly. He put one arm around Lexie's shoulders and used his other hand to wrap her arm around his waist. "Now that you have all the details you need for an in-depth encyclopedia on the subject, may we please get to camp, Miss McKennis?"

Bree lifted her chin so her wings of hair swung back from her face. "Of course," she said, linking her arm through Sally's. "Come on, Sally." They swept on ahead, down the path leading to the check-in booth.

Lexie's heart was racing. Jake's whole side was pressed against hers, and his bare arm was resting lightly on her shoulders, and her arm could feel the muscles in his back through his shirt, and it didn't seem possible that she could be so confused and scared and thrilled at the same time.

"Wait," he whispered, curling his hand around her shoulder until Bree and Sally were out of earshot. As soon as they were, he nudged her forward, keeping his arm in place. "Lexie, that was amazing."

"Oh," she said, turning pink. "It wasn't anything special."

"Seriously?" he said. "I couldn't believe it. I *wish* I were that cool. You should have been a guy. You'd knock the socks off any girl with a move like that."

Lexie started giggling. She couldn't help it. "Knock the socks off?" she said. "How old are you, fifty?"

"Nice," Jake said. "I give you a compliment, and you make fun of me."

"Sorry," Lexie said. "I forgot for a moment that that's really what every girl wants to hear — that she'd make a great boy."

"I *mean*," said Jake, "that you're much smarter than any boy I've ever heard of."

"I'm a girl," Lexie pointed out. "So that's true by definition."

"Dweeb," he said affectionately.

"Loser," she said.

"Smart aleck."

She started giggling again. "Oldest person ever trapped inside a fifteen-year-old."

He pressed one hand to his forehead. "Alas, how my girlfriend abuses me." They'd reached the check-in counter, so he took his arm from around her shoulders and leaned over to sign in.

Lexie glanced around and stopped laughing.

Bree was standing halfway down the path to the swimming pool, her arms folded so her elbows were sharp points at her side. Lexie could practically feel her freezing glare from there.

This wasn't over. Bree wanted Jake, and she thought Lexie was the one standing in her way. The question was, what was Bree going to do about it?

chapter 3

The good news was that the Advanced Tennis class was on a different set of courts, so Jake couldn't see how terribly Lexie played. The bad news was that Sally was in Beginners with Lexie, except she was good, and Lexie really was terrible. Sally's swings were smooth and always connected with the ball. Lexie kept letting go of the tennis racket by accident and nearly beaning the instructor with it. She was pretty sure that Sally was laughing at her, and that tales of Lexie's incompetence would be traveling straight back to Bree.

By lunchtime, Lexie's arms ached and her hair was sticking to her face. She was so relieved when the instructor let them go, she didn't even care that now she'd have to face Bree and Jake again.

Lexie was gathering her stuff when a voice said, "Hey," behind her, and she jumped.

"Sorry to startle you," Sally said, bouncing on

her heels. "I just wanted to say, don't worry, you'll get better. I was pretty bad when I started. I'm still not good enough for Intermediate or Advanced."

Lexie couldn't think of anything interesting to say. "Um. Thanks," she managed.

Sally kept looking at Lexie, as if she was thinking, *How did a girl like you snag Jake Atkinson?* Lexie thought, *I'll answer that if you can tell me why you agreed to be best friends with the scariest girl in school.*

"Well?" Sally said.

"Well what?" Lexie asked.

"Aren't you starving? Let's go to lunch."

Let's? As in "let us"? Us? Me and Sally Kim? There's an us there?

Sally spun her racket impatiently and Lexie quickly grabbed her bag with the hat, the extra sunscreen, and the brown-bag lunch her mom had packed. She followed Sally up the walkway to a bunch of picnic tables under the trees. The other Tennis for Teens campers were gathering there, along with the lifeguard training class from the pool and a group of basketball campers.

Jake was already sitting at a table, unwrapping his lunch. His hair was half-wet from the showers and drying in the sun, so it was kind of spiky and darker than usual. That day his T-shirt was light blue, making his eyes even bluer. He saw Lexie and waved.

"Wow," Sally said. "Did you see his face light up when he saw you? That's so cute. My boyfriend never looks that excited to see me."

Yeah. I guess Jake's a really good actor, Lexie thought.

"You have a boyfriend?" she said, but too quietly, so Sally didn't hear her and she had to repeat herself.

"Oh, sure," Sally said. "Ian Montgomery. Bree set us up in April." That made sense. Ian was athletic and blond and agreeable and would fit in well with Bree's idea of who her friends should date. For one thing, *she'd* never wanted to date him. Anyone she'd dated was off the menu for everyone else.

Sally peeled off to join Bree and her Glare of Death in the line for pizza, and Lexie hesitantly went over to Jake's table. See, this was why Colin should be there. She'd know exactly who to sit with and how. And if she wanted to spend lunchtime reading her book, he wouldn't mind. But of course she had to sit with Jake, right? A girlfriend would normally sit with her boyfriend. That was the normal thing to do.

She set her lunch bag down on the table, opposite him, and he immediately reached out and grabbed it.

"Hey," she said. "Eat your own lunch."

"Sit next to me," he whispered frantically. "Or else *she* will."

Lexie looked up and saw Bree heading purposefully their way. She scooted quickly around the end of the table and managed to sit down next to Jake just before Bree plunked her tray down on the table.

"Oh, Jakey," Bree said, ignoring Lexie, "I saw you playing tennis when I went by the courts earlier. You are *so* talented."

"Thanks," Jake said, opening Lexie's lunch. "Wow, Lexie, your mom really likes carrot sticks, doesn't she?"

"We suspect she owns stock in them or something," Lexie joked. Jake laughed; Bree didn't.

"Not to mention," Bree went on as if they hadn't spoken, "you look so hot in shorts. Not every guy can pull off that look — right, Lexie? It must be so hard for you to concentrate with your *boyfriend* right there looking that hot."

"Oh, we're in two different classes," Lexie said awkwardly.

"So which celebrities do you like, Lexie?" Bree asked. "Any guys as cute as Jake? Don't worry, I'm sure he won't be jealous. Tell me your deep dark secret crush."

Yeah, that would be . . . Jake.

"Um . . . I don't know," Lexie mumbled. "Maybe Jake Gyllenhaal."

Bree rolled her eyes. "Like we haven't all heard *that* one before," she said.

"Here, Lexie," Jake said, and she realized he was saying her name a lot more than usual. He broke his cookie in half and handed her the bigger portion. "To make up for all those carrot sticks."

"Really?" Lexie said. She met his eyes as he handed her the cookie. He looked so worried, she couldn't stop herself from smiling at him.

"That is *so* cute," Sally said, sliding onto the bench, next to Bree. "Ian totally refuses to share his food with me. I once ate a French fry off his plate when he had clearly finished eating, and he, like, didn't speak to me for the rest of the weekend."

"He's probably helping you watch your weight," Bree said nastily. "I'd say he's doing you a favor."

Sally looked hurt. She stared down at her pizza,

poking it with her plastic fork but not eating. Lexie wished she was brave enough to tell Sally that Bree was being crazy — and mean for no reason — but she was too afraid to butt into their conversation. Bree had enough reasons to hate her.

"So what are you going to do for your afternoon activity?" Jake asked Lexie. She realized there were sign-up sheets on all the tables. The list of choices included more tennis (*no, thanks*), learning to papier-mâché (*maybe if I were still eight years old*), Ultimate Frisbee, and pool volleyball. Sadly, going home and watching TV with Colin was not on the list.

"I don't know," Lexie said. "None of this is my idea of fun. I guess Frisbee sounds the least painful."

"Really?" Bree pounced. "I thought for sure you'd want to be with your *boyfriend*. Unless you don't really want to hang out with him, but I'm sure that's not true."

Lexie gave Jake a confused look, and he tapped POOL VOLLEYBALL with one finger. "I'm a team captain," he said. "Cynthia — the woman in charge of pool activities — asked me to because I've had lifeguard training."

"Oh," she said. Now what? On one hand, if

she stuck with Frisbee, she wouldn't be acting like a real girlfriend, would she? But on the other hand . . . pool volleyball meant a bathing suit. In front of Jake and, worse, Bree. At least the red bikini was safely hidden under her bed at home.

"Come on," Jake said, taking one of her hands in both of his. "It'll be fun."

"You don't really want me on your team," Lexie said. "I'm totally terrible."

"I know," Jake said. "I want you on the other guy's team."

Lexie swatted him with her free hand. "That is no way to talk to your girlfriend," she said, forgetting for a moment that Bree was right there, intently watching them.

"You're right," he said. "My apologies, sugar plum. I'm sorry, honey pie. I'll never do it again, my little pumpkin. Is that better?"

She wrinkled her nose at him. "I feel so edible all of a sudden."

"Cute enough to eat," he said. Lexie looked down at the table, turning pink again. He didn't have to overact quite so much. Bree would catch on if he kept being ridiculous.

"Adorable," Sally said, shaking her head. "I aspire to be that adorable."

Bree stood up, grabbed Sally's arm, and yanked her away. As they hurried off, Lexie heard Bree whisper, "*Nauseating,*" just loudly enough for Lexie to hear.

Lexie pulled her hand free and wrapped up the remains of her sandwich. Now that they were gone, how was she supposed to act?

"I think it's going well," said Jake. "Don't you?"

"Um, sure," Lexie said. *In the sense of my not being literally dead yet, anyway.*

"You don't really have to do volleyball if you don't want to," he said.

"That's okay," Lexie said. "I'm sure it'll be fun. Besides, after tennis, I could use a swim."

"Have I said thank you for this?" Jake asked. "Because seriously. Thank you for this."

"I'm not sure I'm helping," Lexie said. "She's still paying so much attention to you."

"I'm sure she'll get over it soon," Jake said. "You won't have to pretend for much longer."

So instead of pretending to date you . . . I can go back to pretending I don't like you.

Lexie sighed. *When do I finally get to stop pretending?*

♥ chapter 4

The girls' changing room by the pool had separate stalls with doors, much to Lexie's relief. She didn't like getting undressed in front of people, plus she was sure Bree and Sally would be staring at her the whole time.

As she waited for a stall, Lexie saw that most of the Beginners tennis class had signed up for pool volleyball, too, including Sally. Bree kept talking loudly about her lifeguard training, like she wanted everyone to know she wasn't a tennis camper like the others. Her sixteenth birthday had been two months before, so she was old enough, and the pool gave special classes for it in the mornings.

Jake would be turning sixteen in a week and a half, more than four months before Colin and Lexie. Lexie wondered suddenly if she was supposed to get him a present. Normally she'd help Colin pick out something funny from both of them, like the *Extreme Worst-Case Scenario Survival Guide*. But as his pretend girlfriend, was she supposed to give him something special and meaningful? Something that Bree would notice, that shouted, "Look, my totally-for-real girlfriend gave me this"?

She'd have to save panicking about that for later. Maybe Colin could help her figure it out. Not for the first time, she wished he was at Summerlodge, too, and she wondered what he was doing all day. Probably beating all her high scores on their games.

She adjusted the straps on her black one-piece and stepped into her flip-flops, tucking the rest of her stuff into her shoulder bag. Her red bead necklace from Jake went carefully into the side zipper pocket, where she was sure it would be safe. The minute she unlatched the door, Bree pulled it open.

"Oh, *Lexie,*" Bree said. "What a *darling* bathing suit. I used to have one just like it. When I was nine."

Bree, of course, was wearing one of her twelve different white bikinis. This one had thin barely-there straps holding up the top, and the bottom was a pair of tiny short-shorts that showed off her long legs. Lexie could not imagine ever, ever, ever wearing something like that in public.

Sally was wearing a two-piece, too, but it was more of a tankini, where the top came all the way down to cover her stomach like a tank top. She kept tugging at it as if trying to make it cover more. It was a deep emerald green with darker green waves across it, and she wore matching emerald-green flip-flops.

"Towels are over there," Sally said, pointing to a folded pile by the door.

"Unless you brought your own," Bree said, "because you don't care for other people's germs." She wound her lavender beach towel around her waist while Sally and Lexie each took one of the plain white ones from the pile. Then she led the way out into the pool area.

Lexie was glad she was wearing waterproof sunscreen, even if her mom was crazy. It was really hot around the pool, like the sun was magnified by the chiseled, fake-looking stones. Up in the two lifeguard stations, two older guys were sitting, looking like Secret Service agents behind their sunglasses. A volleyball net had been set up, stretching across the middle of the pool.

Jake was standing with a couple of freshmen, talking and pointing to the net, but when he spotted Lexie, he broke off and came over to her.

"Hey," he said with a smile. "Long time no see." But Lexie could tell that he was worried about her being alone with Bree in the changing room, and that he was really asking if she was okay.

Before Lexie could say anything, a curly-haired woman in bright yellow culottes blew a whistle around her neck and made them all gather at the wall farthest away from the pool. Then she spent forty-five minutes explaining all the rules of the pool as well as how to play the game. She must have said, "No running on the edge of the pool" five gazillion times. Lexie wasn't sure how she was supposed to take anyone in bright yellow culottes seriously.

Finally she called the team captains forward and read off their assigned teams. Lexie couldn't believe her luck — she was on Jake's team! As she headed over, he high-fived her and winked.

"Did you make that happen?" she whispered.

"Of course," he said. "Cynthia likes me. She's hoping I'll work here as a lifeguard once tennis camp is over."

Best of all, Bree had to be a team captain, too,

and Sally wound up on a third team, so Lexie and Jake didn't have to get too close to them for the rest of the day.

There were six teams, so four teams would watch while the other two played each other, and then they'd switch around. As Cynthia explained it, they'd practice for a week, and then they'd have a tournament the next week to crown a winning team. Lexie realized that that meant she'd signed up for two weeks of pool volleyball. She wouldn't get to switch to something else — like Frisbee — until the two weeks were up. Well, maybe Bree would be over Jake by then.

To her surprise, volleyball was much more fun than she'd expected, although she kept getting water up her nose and a couple of the freshmen on her team were horrifyingly better than she was. She even managed to hit the ball in the right direction a couple of times, and each time she did, Jake yelled, "Yeah!" and splashed her.

Her turn to serve came up. She balanced the ball on one hand and tried to remember what she'd learned in regular volleyball in gym class.

"Here," Jake said, coming up beside her. "Hold this arm out straight." He took her left arm under the water and straightened it out so it was pointing a little to her right. "Now keep that arm straight while you hit it with your other fist." He reached around behind her and touched her right shoulder.

The combination of his hands, her bare arms, and the water made her so nervous, she swung wildly and sent the ball up out of the pool, into the crowd along the edge.

"Don't worry," Jake said, squeezing her shoulder. "You'll get it next time."

Not if you keep helping me like that, I won't! Lexie thought, but the truth was she'd rather be that close to Jake than hit a great volleyball serve any day.

Finally, finally, the end of the day came. Lexie didn't want to face Bree and Sally in the changing room again, so she toweled off her hair, pulled on her shorts over her bathing suit, and headed straight out to the bikes.

A stranger was leaning against the rack, next to her bike. A guy about her age. She'd never seen him before, which probably meant he either was new or went to one of the private schools in town.

"Hey," he said with a lazy, crooked smile. He had amazingly straight white teeth. His hair was shaggy and dark, and his eyes were light brown.

"Um, hi," she said. "Sorry, that's — um, that's my bike."

"Oh, sorry," he said, moving aside. She knelt to unlock it, hoping Jake would come out soon.

"I'm Riley," he said. "I'm just waiting for my brother. Do you go here?"

"Summerlodge?" she said. "Yeah. I'm doing the tennis camp."

"Huh," he said. His eyes had this faraway, dreamy look, and she couldn't tell if he was really listening to her until he turned and smiled at her again. His smile could really catch a girl's attention, even if that girl had a pretend boyfriend she was secretly totally in love with.

"Is it cool?" he said, but kept going without waiting for an answer. "Tennis. Man, I'm bad at tennis."

"Me too," Lexie said. "It's —"

"What did you say your name was?" he asked, shoving his hands in his pockets. He was wearing jeans and a long-sleeved shirt, and she wondered if he was melting in the heat but too cool to admit it.

"I didn't," she said. "Um. It's Lexie." She unwrapped the chain from her bike wheel and stashed it in her shoulder bag. She tried to move

51

as slowly as she could without looking like a mentally challenged alien. She really, really wished Jake would show up. Or else she'd have to stay and make conversation with this strange guy, because of course she couldn't leave without Jake, could she? That wasn't a girlfriendy thing to do.

"Lexie," Riley said. "That's cute. Has anyone ever told you that you look like Sophia Bush?"

"Who's that?"

"Wow, really?" he said. "Or are you just trying to trick me into admitting I watch *One Tree Hill*?"

Lexie giggled. "My brother would kill me if he found that on the TiVo."

"Uh, yeah, me too," Riley said, affecting a deeper voice. "Me, I only watch wrestling. And monster truck rallies. Grrr."

"You're so busted," Lexie said. "Admit it — you stay home whenever *Grey's Anatomy* is on, don't you?"

He laughed, and she found herself smiling despite her nervousness. She liked it when people got her jokes.

"Hey, Lexie," said Jake from behind her. She'd forgotten to keep watching for him, but her heart still leaped into double time as he paused next to her. His T-shirt was slightly damp from his wet hair, so it clung to his shoulders, which were strong from all the swimming and tennis. The light blue color made her want to lean into it, like falling into the sky.

"Who's this?" Jake asked. His gaze was fixed on Riley, and he didn't look too friendly.

"This is Riley," Lexie said, wondering why her voice sounded higher than normal. "We just met. He's waiting for someone."

"Oh," Jake said. Riley reached out his hand, and Jake shook it, the tendons in his arm tensing like he was slamming a hammer down.

"And you are?" Riley said.

"Jake." Pause. "Lexie's boyfriend."

Lexie was astonished. Why on earth did he say that? Bree was nowhere in sight. There was no one around to run back and report to her. There was no reason at all to volunteer that information, as far as she could see. Not that she minded, but it was odd.

"Ah," Riley said.

"We'd better get going, Lexie," Jake said, touching her bike but not looking at her.

"Yeah, okay," she said. She pulled her bike free and stood for a moment awkwardly, waiting for Jake to unlock his bike. Riley was still watching her.

As Jake rolled his bike free, she swung onto hers and said, "Well, see you."

"Nice to meet you, Lexie," Riley said. He gave her the smile again, and she ducked her head and pushed off.

Jake was quiet all the way back to her house. She felt the wind blowing her hair dry and she wondered what he was thinking. At the bottom of her driveway, he braked but stayed straddling his bike.

"Don't you want to come in?" she said. "We can make fun of my lazy slug brother."

"Nah, not today," Jake said. "I've got stuff to do. Tell him I say hi."

"Oh, okay," Lexie said.

He ran his hand along the top of his hair, looking like he was going to say something else, but in the end he just stood up on the pedals and rode away. She watched him ride to the end of the block, where he glanced back and waved at her, and then she rolled her bike into the garage and went into the house.

Colin was lying on the floor in front of the

couch, where she'd expected him to be. As she went into the den, he quickly slid something underneath a pile of cushions.

"What was that?" she said.

"What?" he said, pretending to be focused on a plate on the coffee table. "Here, Mom made snacks. It's basically peanut butter on celery, but cut into slices so it's prettier and harder to eat. Have you ever noticed that she's weird?"

"Colin, come on," Lexie said, flopping down on the couch. "What were you hiding when I came in?"

"Nothing," he said. "Where's Jake?"

Lexie was hurt. Colin never kept anything from her. What could it be?

"Jake decided not to come in," she said. "But he says hi." She waited for a minute, but Colin kept moving the celery around the plate without saying anything.

"So . . . did you have fun today?" she tried. "Tennis was so lame. I'm a total menace with a tennis racket. What did you do?"

"Nothing," he said again.

"I'll bet," she said, reaching for the remote control and flipping the TV to their favorite game.

To her surprise, none of the scores had changed. Either he hadn't played very well that day, or he hadn't played at all.

"Was Bree there?" Colin asked.

"Of course," Lexie said. "She's so scary. And now she seriously hates me."

"But she's really hot," Colin said. "I don't get why Jake wouldn't just date her. *I* would, if I weren't too stupid and boring for her to like me. It sounds a lot easier than pretending to date you."

"Oh, thanks!" Lexie said, pushing herself off the couch. She headed for the door in a huff, but he didn't stop her. In the doorway, she turned and glanced back. He was staring down at the table, rolling a pencil absentmindedly back and forth along the carpet.

Her mom was coming down the stairs as Lexie went up.

"Oh, Lexie!" Mrs. Willis said happily. "How was Summerlodge? Did you have such a lovely time? It wasn't so bad without your brother, was it?"

"It was terrible, like I thought it would be," Lexie said. "And I think something's wrong with Colin. I'm going to take a shower."

Her mom looked disappointed, but she stepped

aside without pressing for more tennis details. At least she didn't ask about the bikini, safely hidden under Lexie's bed.

In her room, Lexie lay down on her bed, feeling tired. It was kind of exhausting being a pretend girlfriend. First there were Bree and Sally; then there was all the complicated Jake stuff, plus that guy Riley; and now Colin was acting strange and keeping secrets. She felt all mixed up, with no one to talk to about it.

And it starts all over again tomorrow.

chapter 5

The next day was even stranger than Lexie had expected, mainly because there was a surprise newcomer to her tennis class. He was leaning against the fence of the tennis courts as she walked up, swinging a racket in one hand.

"Hey, Lexie!" Riley said enthusiastically. "Where's your boyfriend?"

Lexie nearly said, "Who?" but remembered in time. "He's in the Advanced class," she said. "What are you doing here?"

"Well, you made these tennis lessons sound so fun," he said with his crooked smile. "I figured I'd sign up and join in."

"I did?" Lexie tried to remember anything she had said that might possibly have been misunderstood as "tennis is fun."

"Sure," Riley said. "And maybe if you're as bad as I am, we can be partners."

"I'll be pretty impressed if you're as bad as I am," Lexie said.

Sally was on the court already, bouncing a ball off her racket into the air. Lexie wasn't sure, but she got the feeling Sally was watching her and Riley.

"Don't you need to change?" Lexie said as Riley started to follow her through the fence. He was wearing jeans again, although at least he'd switched to a T-shirt.

"I already got the lecture from Sergeant Shorts over there," Riley said, jerking his thumb at Mr. Giambi, the instructor. "But what's he going to do? This is how I am."

"There's a lot of running around," Lexie said worriedly. "Especially when you play with me."

"Don't worry," Riley said, smiling again. "I'll be fine."

He wasn't fine. By 10:00 A.M., when they switched from drills to practice matches, he was sweating so much that his shirt stuck to his back, and he looked exhausted. Lexie felt bad for him, so when they were paired up, she tried to be the one to run after the ball as much as possible. Each time she did, he would collapse down on the court and lie there until Mr. Giambi yelled at him to get up.

He was right about one thing, though: He was really bad at tennis, too. He had trouble even getting it over the net, so she hardly ever got to try volleying it back.

Finally, for the last hour, Mr. Giambi switched the partners and she was paired with Sally. At least with a good partner she had a better chance to practice, but Riley seemed disappointed that they were split up. She glanced over at his court a couple of times and caught him watching her instead of the tennis ball he was supposed to be watching.

"Hey," Sally said during a break for water. "I've been meaning to talk to you."

It was funny how a simple sentence like that could make a person so nervous. Lexie screwed the cap back on her water bottle, trying to look calm.

"This Friday," Sally went on, "would you and Jake want to go on a double date with me and Ian?"

"Really?" Lexie said. That was about the furthest thing from what she'd expected Sally to say. A double date? A real date? With Bree's best friend? *Maybe that's why,* the voice in her head whispered. *Bree's assigned her to spy on us. To see if Jake and I still act like a couple away from Summerlodge. So I have to say yes, don't I?*

"Um," she said, hedging. "Let me ask Jake. But thanks, that sounds like fun."

"It would be fun," Sally said. "I was thinking we could just walk downtown to the movie theater on Main Street — I think they have the new Pixar movie there, which Ian is being kind of a jerk about seeing, but I'll get him to go. And then we could have dinner at the diner across the street afterward."

Lexie nodded. Sally added, "Unless you want to do something else. My mom could drive us to the mall, but I thought we'd have more fun if we could go somewhere without any parents yakking at us the whole way. Ian's not a big fan of my mom."

"The one in town sounds fine," said Lexie. "I've been wanting to see the Pixar movie, too."

"*Finding Nemo* was *so* funny," Sally said, and Lexie would have agreed, but Mr. Giambi called them back to the court to keep practicing.

On the way to lunch, Riley caught up with Lexie and Sally.

"Okay," he said, "lesson learned. No more jeans. I'm afraid you're going to think my cool factor is plummeting, but you know, if the choice is shorts or death, I guess shorts wins by a tiiiiiny margin."

"I won't think you're less cool," Lexie said.

"I'll think you're a heck of a lot smarter," Sally said. "Hi, I'm Sally."

"Riley," he said.

"Oh, Lexie," Sally said, "I forgot to mention — don't say anything to Bree about our double date. I'll tell her later, but she can be weird about stuff like that."

Clever, Lexie thought. *Make me think Bree doesn't know about it when she's really the one who masterminded the whole thing.*

"No problem," she said.

"Double date?" Riley said.

"Maybe," Lexie answered. "I have to check with Jake."

"Oh, right," Riley said. "Your boyfriend."

They got in sight of the picnic tables, and once again, Jake was already there. He raised his hand to wave to Lexie but stopped when he saw Riley.

"And there he is," Riley said.

"You can, um, sit with us, if you want," Lexie said.

"Great, thanks," he said. "First, hot dogs." He

headed off toward the lunch line. Sally raised her eyebrows at Lexie and followed him. Lexie wondered if that was a girl-code expression that a normal girl would have been able to translate. With a sigh, she headed over to Jake.

This time she remembered to sit next to him instead of across from him. He smiled at her as she sat down, and it was such a different smile from Riley's. It made her calmer instead of more nervous, and it said, *I'm happy to see you,* instead of, *I know something about you.* He smelled sharp and clean, like apple shampoo.

"Hi there, girlfriend," he said as she sat down. She wondered how long he was going to find that funny, but she liked the way he said it, kind of warm and teasing at the same time. She was glad to see he seemed to be in a better mood than he had been when he'd dropped her off the day before.

"Hey," he added, "you're wearing the necklace I got you." He reached out and touched one of the glass beads. His fingers brushed the side of her neck like a whisper of wind, and her heart sped up. Hadn't he ever noticed that she wore it all the time?

"Yeah," she said awkwardly. "I love it."

"That's so cool," he said, removing his hand. "Go, me. What do you have for lunch today?"

"I, um," Lexie said, clearing her throat, "well, I'm guessing more carrot sticks."

Jake laughed, but then his face changed, closing down again. Lexie turned to see Riley sitting down on the other side of her.

"Hi," Jake said. "I thought you didn't go here."

"I do now," Riley said. "Hello again, Lexie's boyfriend."

Bree and Sally plunked their trays down on the other side of the table, and Lexie was almost pleased to see them. She felt a weird tension between Riley and Jake, and sitting in between them made her nervous.

"Hi there," Bree said, leaning toward Riley like a leopard sniffing out prey. "I'm Bree. I'm a lifeguard, or I will be soon."

"Hey, Bree," Riley said. "A lifeguard? That's awesome."

"Yes, well," Bree said, shooting a look at both Lexie and Sally, "I thought it would be a good way to help my community. Better than tennis, for instance."

"Oh, I'm doing tennis," Riley said, and Lexie nearly giggled at the "oops" look on Bree's face.

"Really," Bree purred. "Sally, you didn't tell me about any gorgeous guys in your tennis class."

"He just started today," Sally said, stabbing a fork into her salad like she was hoping it would die and turn into a hamburger.

"And what's your name, handsome?" Bree asked.

"Riley," he said. "What's yours?"

She wrinkled her nose like she was trying to hide her real expression. "I already told you," she said. "It's Bree."

"Oh, right," he said. He gave Lexie a huge obvious wink. It took her a minute to realize he was saying, *The one we're not telling about the double date.*

Which reminded her. But she couldn't ask Jake there, in front of everyone. "Hey," she said, turning to him. He was moodily shredding her brown paper bag. "Um, Jake. I forgot to get a soda. Want to come with me to . . . um . . . buy one?"

Jake looked confused. He knew her mom didn't like her to drink soda. When he paused, Riley jumped in. "I'll come with you," he said. "I've got tons of change for the vending machine."

"No, that's okay," Jake said quickly. "I can buy

my own girlfriend a soda, thanks." He took Lexie's hand and tugged her away from the bench. His hand was cooler than hers, and much bigger.

As they walked away, Lexie heard Bree purr, "You can buy *me* a soda, Riley."

"Nah, I'm good," he said.

Lexie hid a smile. Bree wasn't going to like that! But maybe if she turned her attention to Riley, she'd lose interest in Jake and leave him and Lexie alone.

"What kind do you want?" Jake said, feeding quarters into the slot.

"Cherry Coke," she said. "I can pay for it, Jake."

"No, no," he said, waving her hand away. "Let me, since I don't have a cookie to split with you today." He grinned at her, then glanced over her shoulder, back at the table. "I don't like that guy," he said, punching the Cherry Coke button a little too hard.

"Riley?" Lexie said. "Why?"

"Well, why didn't he start tennis camp at the same time as the rest of us?" Jake said. "Why doesn't he have any of his own friends? And his smile is all lopsided."

"That's true," Lexie said. "He is a little weird — he wore jeans to tennis this morning. But he seems nice enough."

"Hmm," Jake said, turning to head back.

"Wait," she said, catching his sleeve. "Actually, I needed to ask you something."

"Aha," he said. "I thought the soda thing was out of the blue."

"Well, if you help me drink it, I figure I'll only be half breaking my mom's rule, right?" He smiled, and she told him about Sally's double date offer. "I know it's strange," Lexie said. "Maybe we could tell her you already have plans, or that our parents won't let us go, or something."

"Are you sure?" Jake said. "I think it could be fun, don't you?"

"Oh," Lexie said, "well, I mean, if you —"

"Why not, right?" Jake said. "I want to see it; you want to see it."

"But with Sally and Ian?"

"Well, we don't have to talk to them during the movie. But we also don't have to go," he said. "I mean, if you don't want to, I can totally say no for us. I'm sure you don't want to go on your first date with a guy who's just a friend, like me, right?"

He was looking at her really intently. *You have no idea,* she thought. *I want to go on my first date with you, plus every other date for the rest of my life.*

"No, I mean, sure," she said. "We can go. Let's do it. Besides, if Bree is behind it, this should help convince her we're really dating, right?"

"Right," he said. "That's why we're doing it. Of course."

When they got back to the table, Bree was explaining lifeguard training to Riley, who looked fascinated. Sally looked bored, but when Lexie caught her eye and gave her a thumbs-up, her face brightened.

"I'll call you," she mouthed while Bree wasn't looking.

The afternoon went a lot like the previous afternoon, except that Riley joined pool volleyball and was put on Bree's team. Seeing him in his swimsuit made Lexie realize why he liked jeans better than shorts: His legs were thin and paler than his arms, which looked sort of odd. But he turned out to be a lot better at this sport than tennis, and he made a lot of energetic leaps and dives to hit the ball, splashing everyone around the pool in the process. Whenever he saw Lexie watching him, he gave her his crooked smile.

At the end of the day, Jake hustled out of the changing room almost as soon as he went in, catching up to Lexie while she was still on the path to the bikes.

"Hey," she said. "That was fast."

"That guy was annoying me," Jake said. "He keeps asking questions about our relationship, like how long we've been dating and stuff."

"Really?" Lexie said. "That's weird. I wonder why."

"Uh, yeah," Jake said, spinning the combination lock on his bike. "Weird. Let's go before he comes out."

As they rode back to Lexie's house, she wondered if she should talk to Jake about Colin. Maybe he could help her figure out what was wrong with her twin brother. She decided to wait and see if Jake noticed anything himself. But when he came inside with her, Colin seemed more cheerful than he had the day before. The three of them spent the rest of the afternoon trying to set up and film gory special effects from a book Jake had found. It didn't work very well; they ended up with ketchup all over the kitchen and several bits of carrot that didn't look anything like severed fingers.

"Better luck tomorrow," Jake said, heading out the door. "See you in the morning, Lexie." She stood at the screen door and waved as he pedaled away. Thorn and Alanna nosed their way into the kitchen and snuffled across the floor, licking up spattered ketchup and carrot bits.

"Oh, dear," Mrs. Willis said, coming into the kitchen. "I gather we're having takeout for dinner."

"We're cleaning it up," Colin said. "Don't worry."

"I'm quite sure you are," his mom said. "Lexie, Sally Kim is on the phone for you. When you're done, ask her if I can speak to her mother."

Colin gave Lexie a curious look. He knew as well as she did that a phone call from Sally Kim was not at all the normal event their mother seemed to think it was.

Lexie picked up Alanna for moral support, took the portable phone into her room, and shut the door.

"Hi, Sally," she said into the phone, lying down on the bed. Alanna curled up beside her and began licking her fingers with energetic snorting sounds.

"Hey, Lexie," Sally said, as if she called her

every day. "So let's figure out Friday. Ian's being a pain about it because he's going on a camping trip with his family the next day or something. But he'll come. It'll be fun, don't you think?"

"Sure," Lexie said.

"I've been wanting to go on a double date for ages," Sally said, "but Bree hates them. She likes to keep her boyfriends to herself. Anyway, I don't really want Ian to model himself on any of her relationships. But I figure he could pick up some tips from Jake, right? I'd love it if he treated me a bit more like Jake treats you."

Lexie thought that was funny. The whole time Jake had been dating Amy Sorrento, Amy had complained nonstop (Jake's words) about what an unenthusiastic, uninspired, boring, neglectful boyfriend he was (her words). Maybe he was just better at pretending to be in a relationship than at actually being in one.

"Are you excited?" Sally asked. "Dinner and a movie, totally romantic, right? Is it okay if I have my mom drop me off at your place beforehand, so we can walk together? It's closer from your house."

"Yeah, okay," Lexie said, and then, because

she felt bad about how excited Sally seemed (even if it was a trick), she added, "I'm excited for this movie."

"Me *too*," Sally said, and that started her off on a comparison of *Cars* and *Monsters, Inc.* They ended up talking for half an hour — well, Sally did most of the talking — and by the time Lexie got back downstairs, Colin had finished cleaning the kitchen. Mrs. Willis was standing at the counter, sorting takeout menus.

"Here you go, Mom," Lexie said, handing her the phone.

"Oh, thanks, Lexie," her mom said. "Pick a menu and order, would you? You both know what your father and I like. He should be home from work in about half an hour." Mr. Willis took a train to the city every morning before the rest of his family got up, and often came home late at night. Lexie didn't understand exactly what he did — something to do with numbers and law and banks and contracts.

As soon as Mrs. Willis had wandered out of the kitchen, chatting away with Mrs. Kim, Lexie pulled herself up to sit on the counter and whispered, "Colin, guess what?"

"I don't get it," he said, studying a carrot.

"Why did it look so fake? We were using the black-and-white setting, so it's not the color. Even I'm not dumb enough to think we can get away with bright orange fingers."

"Colin, listen," Lexie insisted. "I'm going on a date on Friday."

That did get his attention, if only for a moment. He put the carrot down and picked up the pile of menus. Thorn butted at his knees, demanding more carrot pieces with a small woof.

"With who?" Colin asked.

"With Jake, of course," Lexie said. "Remember the traumatizing soap opera you volunteered me for?" *Which you haven't even asked me about. Like you don't care if Bree McKennis murders me in my sleep.*

"Oh," he said, sounding relieved. "So it's just a pretend date."

"Well, it's a double date with Sally Kim and Ian Montgomery," Lexie said. "But, Colin, I have no idea what I'm supposed to do. Or say. Or *wear.* Oh my *God.*"

"Who cares?" Colin said. "It's just Jake. He doesn't care what you wear."

Sadly true, Lexie thought. "Okay," she said, "but Sally will be reporting right back to Bree. So

73

I have to at least pretend to care." *That's my story, anyway. So Colin doesn't notice how much I actually do care.*

"You'll figure it out," Colin said. "You don't need your dumb brother's help. I vote for Indian or Mexican. You decide."

He dropped two menus on the counter next to her and left the room, Thorn and Alanna pattering along behind him. Lexie stared at the door. What on earth was wrong with Colin?

chapter 6

Colin wasn't the only one acting bizarre. Mrs. Willis kept giving Lexie tiny smiles all through dinner Tuesday night. On Wednesday she left a pile of nail polish and makeup on Lexie's desk. And on Thursday evening she suggested a shopping trip, "just us girls," even though she knew Lexie hated shopping. Lexie wasn't about to be bossed into tennis *and* shopping in one week, so she said no.

"Are you sure, sweetheart?" her mom said. "We could get you something nice to wear. In case you need it sometime soon. For anything."

Aha. Lexie's mom was on to her. Mrs. Kim must have told her about the double date. Lexie was kind of impressed that her mom had managed not to ask Lexie a million questions right away.

"Oh, no, I don't need anything," Lexie said. Her mom's face fell, and Lexie felt a twinge of guilt. "Besides, Mom," she added, trying to be nice, "you're a much better shopper than I am. I like the stuff you get me." It was true. With the exception of the bikini, Mrs. Willis's taste in clothes was remarkable. Sometimes Lexie thought it was the only thing keeping her out of the ranks of the true dorks of the school.

"All right," Mrs. Willis said, hovering in the doorway. "If you're sure."

"Uh-huh," Lexie said. "Thanks."

As her mom closed the door, Lexie crawled over the bed and knocked three times on the wall, the signal for Colin to come over. Then she started pulling clothes out of her closet.

"What?" Colin said, opening the door and poking his head around.

"Come help me decide what to wear tomorrow," Lexie said.

"No way," Colin said.

"Colin!"

"That's girl stuff."

"And where am I supposed to find a girl to help me with this?" Maybe if Karina weren't all the way in *China* . . . although Karina had never really cared about clothes, either.

Colin shrugged. "Ask Mom."

"Yeah, right," Lexie said. "So, should I lie to

her and say I'm suddenly dating Jake, who's been our friend for three years, or should I explain that I'm only *pretend* dating him to protect him from another girl? Which of those fantastic stories do you think she'd like best?"

"Whatever," Colin said. "I see skirts, so I'm leaving."

"Colin!" But he had already shut the door with a firm click.

Lexie hesitated, looking at the scattered hangers and folds of fabric. Was this a fancy date? The diner wasn't exactly a fancy place. So was it more of a jeans and T-shirt event? She didn't want to look like she'd made too much effort, but she didn't want to underdress, either. She tried to remember the time difference in China. But her parents had set strict rules about when and for how long she could talk to Karina, and their next phone date wasn't for another week. She'd have to find her girly advice elsewhere.

Her hands shook a little as she picked up the phone and dialed. Sure, Sally was probably only doing this date thing because Bree told her to. But she couldn't lie about what she was going to wear. So maybe her advice could be useful, in just this one situation.

"Oh, howdy-*doo*, Lexie," Mrs. Kim said with the significant emphasis one might use to say, "You *are* the next president of the United States." "Hold on, let me get Sally."

"Lexie!" Sally cried as she picked up. "I'm so glad you called! I was just freaking out because I have no idea what to wear tomorrow."

"Really?" Lexie said, her nervousness evaporating. "That's why I called you!"

"Oh, *awesome*," Sally said. "Okay. Describe every single item of clothing you own, and then I'll do the same, and then we'll pick outfits that will look good next to each other but won't look like they deliberately match, and then we'll panic and pick backup outfits, and then we'll change them around, and then we'll throw out the whole plan and start over."

Lexie laughed. "All right, you asked for it," she said. "But I own a lot of clothes. My mom *loves* shopping."

"You're lucky," Sally said. "Mine will never take me. And you guys have great malls around here; in my old town there was, like, one, and it was a whole hour away. I could spend my life in a mall, couldn't you?"

"Um," Lexie said. "Well . . ."

"We'll go together sometime," Sally said. "I'll bet it's a lot more fun with someone who doesn't always answer the question 'Does this make me look fat?' with 'Actually, your *fat* makes you look fat.' I think Bree got that from a movie, but she thinks it's *so* funny."

"That is crazy," Lexie said, feeling a lot braver now that Bree wasn't there to hear her. "Sally, you don't need to lose weight. You're way thinner than I am."

"Yeah, but you're cute like that," Sally said. "You have curves. My extra weight just makes me look thicker instead of curvier."

"Sally, seriously," Lexie said. "That is crazy talk."

"Well, start with your tops," Sally said, changing the subject. "Do you have anything red?"

"Sure," Lexie said, and Sally laughed.

"I'm kidding, Lexie," she said. "You wear red, like, every day."

"I do?"

"I'm surprised your bathing suit isn't red," Sally said.

"Maybe if I ever get a second one," Lexie said. "But I like the one I have."

"Doesn't it get boring wearing the same one

every day?" Sally had three that she'd been cycling between, two tankinis and a one-piece.

"No — I mean, I like it," Lexie said.

"That's the important thing," Sally said. "So, tops. How about green for a change?"

Finally, an hour later, they had decided that Lexie would wear a gray shirt and a black skirt with sandals that were comfortable enough to walk a few blocks in, while Sally would wear a sky-blue sundress.

Lexie fell asleep feeling much happier, even though she was still mad at Colin for being so unhelpful.

The next morning, as she was detaching her tennis racket from her bike, Jake suddenly grabbed her hand.

"Are you excited for our date tonight, Lexie?" he said, a little bit too loudly.

"Shh," Lexie said, glancing around for Bree. But the only person she saw was Riley, strolling across the parking lot a few feet away from them. He gave her a wave-salute and headed in through the gates.

"Is it a secret from Riley, too?" Jake said, still holding on to her hand.

"No," she said. "I was just making sure Bree

wasn't around. Ironic, right? I mean, we're going on this date to prove that we're dating, but we're keeping it secret from the person we're proving it to. Who knew deception could be so complicated?"

"It is funny," he said. "So are you? Excited?"

How was she supposed to answer this? "Are you?" she asked.

"I asked you first." He smiled, but there was a small dent above one of his eyebrows that he got only when he was worried.

"Sure I am," she said. "Don't worry about it, Jake; we'll have fun."

"It's just, this is the part where my last three girlfriends . . . okay, my only three girlfriends . . . usually started to get mad at me," Jake said. "Like, because I'm not calling enough, or complimenting them enough, or giving them enough presents, or something."

"You don't have to do any of that," Lexie said, shaking her head. Lowering her voice, she added, "This is just pretend, remember?"

"I know," he said, looking down at her hand in his. "But — if it were real, would you want me — I mean, whoever your real boyfriend was — to do all that stuff?"

"I don't know," Lexie said truthfully. "Not if it's work. It shouldn't be hard. I wouldn't want you — I mean, him — to only be complimenting me because I asked for it, you know? Or because you think you have to. I mean, I think if someone wanted to date me, I'd be happy with whatever they wanted to do to show it." She shrugged.

"That's what I figure," Jake said. They started walking up the path into Summerlodge. She wondered if he remembered that he was still holding her hand. "Although I guess if it were the right girl, I'd want to do all that stuff. So maybe Amy was right about me."

"Nuh-uh," Lexie said loyally. "She didn't appreciate you." *Not like I would.*

"Oh, look, it's the lovebirds," Bree said, popping out from behind the check-in booth. She stretched, showing off her perfectly flat, tan stomach between her shirt and short skirt. For once, she was wearing a color other than white — a light blue fitted shirt. "So what are you guys doing tonight?" she said in her low, silky voice. "To celebrate your one-week anniversary? Or did you celebrate it on Wednesday, ha-ha?"

"We have plans," Jake said.

"Private plans?" Bree said. "Or maybe we could double-date. Because I was thinking of asking that guy Riley out." Confusingly, she and Jake both glanced at Lexie as she said this.

"Oh, I don't —" Lexie started to stammer.

"Sorry," Jake said. "Private plans."

Bree narrowed her eyes. "Doing what?"

"It's a surprise for Lexie," Jake said. *Smart,* Lexie thought.

"Hmm." Bree sniffed. "All right, you can tell me later, Jake. It can be our little secret." She ran her manicured fingers down his arm and he twitched away.

Bree tossed back her pale blond wings of hair and stared at Lexie while Jake signed in. Lexie balanced one foot on top of the other sneaker, feeling uneasy. Bree's gaze traveled up and down, examining every inch of Lexie.

"What's that?" Bree said suddenly, darting forward and plucking at Lexie's necklace.

"It's my necklace," Lexie said, falling back.

"You wear it all the time," Bree said. "Even when it totally doesn't go with your outfit. Like today." After what Sally had said, Lexie had decided to dig out a shirt that wasn't red. And it was true: The dark purple color of her T-shirt didn't exactly match the glowing ruby red of the beads.

"It's — Jake gave it to me," Lexie mumbled.

"Awww," Bree said. "Only a week and already you're giving her jewelry? What a dashing boyfriend you are, Jakey. I hope your girlfriend is good enough for you. Kidding!"

"I gave it to her a while ago," Jake said. "Back when I was starting to figure out I liked her but didn't know what to do about it yet."

Lexie thought she must be turning the same color as the beads. If only that were actually true!

"I have to get to tennis," she blurted, and took off at a sprint for the courts. Jake would have to handle the rest of the morning's interrogation without her.

Riley was warming up outside the fence by jogging in place. He had showed up on Wednesday in jean shorts that were clearly just jeans he'd cut the legs off of, but now he was wearing real shorts.

"Hey, Lexie," he said. "Remember how we were talking about *Lost* yesterday?" She vaguely remembered saying something about liking the show, but she wouldn't have called it a whole

84

conversation. He rattled on without waiting for her to answer. "Well, they're having a marathon tonight on TV, and I thought maybe we could watch it together, so you can explain it to me and maybe I'll see how good it is. Whatcha think? We could order pizza."

"Oh, that sounds like fun, Riley," Lexie said. "But I'm going out with Jake tonight. Sorry." She was half sorry and half not. She loved watching *Lost,* but it sounded a bit intimidating, just her and Riley hanging out.

"Awww," Riley said. "Sure you don't want to ditch him? This is the only night the marathon will be on!"

"I can't do that," Lexie said. "But I can loan you the DVDs of Season One, if you want."

"I'd rather watch it with you," Riley said. "What are you doing with Jake tonight, anyway?"

"We're going to the movies in town," Lexie said.

Riley looked like he was going to try again to convince her, but just then Sally came up, linked her arm through Lexie's, and tugged her away, whispering about plans for that night.

It wasn't until later, during lunch, that something occurred to Lexie. Had Riley been asking her on a date? TV and pizza wasn't a typical date . . . and he knew about Jake . . . but some people would call that a date. It was certainly the first time a boy had asked her to do something with just him.

What would she have said if she weren't pretend dating Jake? Would she want to date Riley? *But I don't like him that way,* Lexie thought. *Do I? He doesn't make me all fizzy inside the way Jake does. He makes me nervous . . . but maybe that's what it's supposed to feel like, meeting a new guy you like.*

She didn't want to date anyone but Jake. But if Jake didn't want to date her — and Riley did — maybe she should try it, for the experience. *I shouldn't be the only girl in high school who's never been kissed.* The thought of kissing Riley gave her butterflies in her stomach.

Well, it doesn't matter, anyway, she told herself firmly. *He thinks I'm dating Jake. And now that I've turned him down once, I doubt he'll ask again.* She glanced sideways at his shaggy mane of hair and his large hands. On her other side, Jake leaned forward to grab a napkin. His arm touched hers, and then stayed there, his skin brushing hers, for the rest of lunch.

Riley kept looking at her and trying to make

her laugh. He even stole a couple of her carrot sticks. And every time she looked up, Lexie found Bree glaring at her. Bree had been flirting with Riley all week, but he didn't seem to have noticed. She'd even been ignoring Jake in favor of Riley, but all Riley's attention was fixed on Lexie. This surprised her as much as it did Bree. If he spent one day at Carlisle High, he'd realize the difference in their social status, and then surely he'd lose interest in Lexie immediately.

She sort of wished he would. She didn't like the way Bree looked at her — as if Lexie had stolen *two* of Bree's boys, and now she would have to pay . . . one way or another.

She was able to push Riley and Bree out of her mind as she biked home with Jake. Their date was only a few hours away! Even a pretend date was worlds more exciting than sitting at home with her parents and Colin for another Friday night, especially with her brother's ongoing weirdness.

"I'll be back at six," Jake said, pausing in the driveway. "With my tuxedo pressed and shoes shined."

"I should hope so," Lexie said. "My ball gown wouldn't go with anything else."

He grinned and saluted as she wheeled her bike into the garage.

"Hello?" she called as she went into the house. "Colin?"

"He's at the library," Mrs. Willis said, popping out of the den. "How was your day? Is the tennis getting more fun?"

Lexie shrugged. "Not really. But I think I'm getting better at pool volleyball." She'd actually gotten a couple of serves over the net. Jake had whooped and hollered, and Riley had applauded from the sidelines. Even Sally had given her a thumbs-up.

Lexie's mother hovered for a minute, as if she were waiting for something to happen.

"Mom?" Lexie said. "Are you okay?"

"Of course I am," Mrs. Willis said. "Don't you want to go upstairs and drop off your things?"

Lexie glanced down at her shoulder bag and tennis racket. "Yeah, okay. I thought I'd get a glass of water first."

"I'll get it," Mrs. Willis said, bolting for the kitchen. "You go upstairs."

"Mom, you're being bizarre!" Lexie called after her. Shaking her head, she headed up the stairs and dropped her stuff inside her room.

Hanging from the hook on the outside of her closet was a dress. It was a shimmering burnt orange color, like autumn leaves, with a V-neck, a dropped waist, and thin ribbons of darker red around the waist and the knee-length hem. Lexie touched it in awe. The fabric was soft and shiny but not clingy.

"Do you like it?" her mother asked from the doorway.

"Wow, Mom," Lexie said. "I mean — wow."

"I hope it fits," Mrs. Willis said, sitting down on Lexie's bed.

"Let's find out," Lexie said, slipping it off the hanger. It rustled like autumn leaves, too, as she slid it on. Her mom came over to help her zip up the back. It fit perfectly.

"How do you do that?" Lexie said, spinning in front of the mirror. "It's amazing."

"Well, I just thought you should have something special for your first date," Mrs. Willis said, and then clapped her hands over her mouth. "Oh! I wasn't going to say anything!"

"That's okay," Lexie said. She wanted to tell her mom the truth, but wouldn't her mom be disappointed that she'd gone to so much trouble for a fake date?

"I've been hoping you'd tell me about it yourself," Mrs. Willis said.

"Well, we're trying not to make it a big deal," Lexie said, feeling awkward.

"I understand," her mom said, getting up and heading to the door. "I just want you to know — I've always thought you and Jake would make a perfect couple." She beamed at Lexie as she shut the door behind her.

Yeah, me too, Lexie thought. *Now somebody tell Jake that.*

chapter 7

The first thing Lexie did was call Sally to tell her that her outfit had changed, which it turned out Sally had been planning as well. Then Lexie showered, blow-dried her hair, put on her neck-lace and her vanilla-scented perfume that she almost never wore, painted her toenails dark red, and dressed. At six o'clock, she was sitting on the edge of a chair in the den, trying not to wrinkle her dress, even though her mother said the fabric was supposed to be wrinkle-proof.

"I told you that you didn't have to dress up so much," Colin said from his prone position on the couch. "Jake will think it's weird."

"No, he won't," Lexie snapped. Of course, this was what she'd been worrying about for the last two hours. But it was too late now.

The doorbell rang, and she leaped up to answer it before her mother could get there.

It was Sally. She squealed the instant she saw Lexie.

"Oh my goodness! You look fantastic!"

"Come in," Lexie said, blushing. "Jake's not here yet."

"What a hero your boyfriend is," Sally said. "My loser said he'd meet us there. Which means, by the way, that he'll have already bought his ticket, and I'll have to buy my own. Ian's a little unclear on some of the basic principles of dating."

Lexie hadn't thought about that. Would Jake be paying for her? Maybe he'd have to, for appearances, and then she could pay him back later.

"Hi, Colin," Sally said as they entered the den. "Hey, did I see you at the drugstore yesterday?"

"No," he said quickly.

"I thought it was you," Sally said, "but I couldn't figure out why anyone would be buying notebooks and a protractor in the summertime, so maybe I was wrong."

Lexie gave Colin a puzzled look, but he didn't meet her eyes.

The doorbell rang again, and this time it was Jake. He looked freshly showered and his short-sleeved gray button-down made his eyes look all smoky and dark. He was holding a short, dark red rose.

"Holy smokes," he said. "You — that — you — uh . . . I like your dress."

Lexie felt like she must be turning the world's brightest shade of red.

"Hi, Jake," she managed.

"This is for you," he said, handing her the rose. As she took it, their fingers brushed, and suddenly he leaned forward and kissed her on the cheek. It was soft and quick, like a butterfly bumping against her face. Guessing that that meant Sally was behind her, Lexie glanced around, but they were alone in the hallway.

So . . . why did he — ?

"Jake!" Colin called from the den. "Stop loitering and come in here!"

"Thank you," Lexie whispered, shutting the door behind Jake as he stamped his feet on the welcome mat. He looked quizzical, and she held up the flower.

"Oh my God," Sally said, poking her head in. "Did you get her that, Jake? That's unbelievable. Do you know how many times Ian has gotten me flowers? *Zero*. He's such a troglodyte. That was the Word of the Day today; isn't it cool? Man, look how perfect that rose is! You guys are too cute for words. Lexie, let's go find something to put it in." She fastened her hand around Lexie's wrist and dragged her into the kitchen. Jake went into the den and Lexie could hear the murmur of his voice and Colin's.

"How much does that guy adore you?" Sally said, pulling open cabinets. "I know Amy Sorrento a little from field hockey and I don't think he ever got her flowers. I'm sorry, I shouldn't bring up the ex-girlfriend, should I? Don't worry, he never looked at her the way he looks at you. Oh, here, this should work." She fished out a small glass vase and helped Lexie fill it with water.

Lexie set the rose in the vase and gently touched the petals. It *was* perfect. Why couldn't this all be real?

They said good-bye to Colin and set off walking. Sally chattered most of the way, so Lexie didn't have to worry about what to say to Jake. Normally it was easy to talk to him, but this was different. This was a date. Sort of.

Ian Montgomery was standing in front of the movie theater, rocking on his heels. Unlike Jake, he was just wearing a T-shirt and ripped jeans, and he looked like he hadn't showered in a couple of days. He also didn't compliment Sally, although Lexie thought she looked totally cute in her dark green sundress. And Sally had been right: He'd already bought his ticket, so she had to buy her own. Jake closed his hand over Lexie's as she tried to pull money out of her purse.

"No, no," he said. "Let me do the boyfriend thing." He grinned and she smiled back.

"*Ahem*," Sally said. "The *boyfriend* thing, you say? You mean, taking your girlfriend to the movies, bringing her flowers, telling her she looks nice? Are there boyfriends who actually *do* that?"

"Hey, I'm here, aren't I?" Ian said grumpily. "Even though this movie looks super lame. You should be happy enough about that."

"Oh, I am," Sally said, taking his hand. "I feel so *blessed* to be *honored* with your *presence,* I can't even handle it."

Lexie giggled, but Ian huffed out a breath of air like he didn't get that she was joking.

Inside, there was a confusing moment as they figured out where to sit. But Lexie wound up between Jake and Sally, with Ian on the other side of Sally. Then Jake offered to go get popcorn, and

Ian asked him to get some for him, too. When Jake came back, he was also carrying a large soda and a box of Junior Mints for Lexie.

"You like these, right?" he said to her as he sat down.

"They're my favorite, thank you," she said. On her other side, Sally sighed loudly, but Ian missed her meaningful look.

"I figured we could split the soda," Jake said, "but, um, they were nearly out of straws, so I only took one. Is that gross? Do you mind?"

"No, that's okay," Lexie said. As she took a sip, she realized it was Cherry Coke, the kind she liked. Jake was a perfect pretend boyfriend. He should take notes for the next time he really dated someone. She looked down at her hands, suddenly feeling sad. She didn't want him to date anyone else. She didn't want to go back to being just Lexie while someone else got to be Jake's girlfriend. And then Sally would pity her, and Bree would be so smug.

The lights went down and Jake leaned over. "Are you all right?" he whispered. "The soda seemed to really depress you."

She laughed. "Well, it had such a sad childhood," she whispered back. "I feel like we're taking advantage of it."

"Nah, just putting it out of its misery," Jake said with a grin, and then the previews came on.

As the theater went totally dark and the movie started, Lexie began to wonder what to do with her hands. Should she rest them on her knees? Or on the armrest? Or fold them in front of her? Or cross her arms? Was Jake thinking about holding her hand? She slid her eyes sideways without moving her head and saw that Sally and Ian were holding hands. Would Sally notice if she and Jake didn't? Should she do something, or wait for Jake to do something, or —

Jake reached over and took her hand, resting it on top of his on the armrest.

Okay. That answered that question. Of course, he'd been on dates like this before. He knew the right thing to do. Lexie glanced sideways again and saw that Ian and Sally were kissing. (!!!) And the movie had barely started! Surely they wouldn't expect her and Jake to do that. Would they?

An unfamiliar sensation brushed across her hand, and she nearly jumped out of her seat. Jake was slowly running his thumb back and forth over her knuckles. It felt like a secret code vibrating through her skin. Almost as if he were saying, "Don't worry, I'm here," and, "You're beautiful," and, "I can't resist you." Why was he doing that? What did it mean? Should she do something, too?

Lexie knew she was being crazy, but her heart was ignoring her brain and had sped up to a million beats an hour. She could barely concentrate on the movie. Luckily it was a pretty short one, because by the end she didn't think her heart could take any more.

"Wasn't that great?" Sally enthused as the crowd spilled out into the street. "I knew it would be great. It was so great!"

Lexie wondered how Sally could have enjoyed the movie when she seemed to have spent so much of it kissing Ian. Then Sally stopped in her tracks, and Ian had to drag her out of the way of the people behind her.

"Oh, *no,*" Sally moaned. "What is *she* doing here?"

Bree was standing outside the movie theater, arms folded. She looked long and slim and elegant, as always, although the angry expression made her much less pretty.

"Sally!" she hissed.

"Hey, Bree," Sally said nervously. "Look who we ran into."

"After all I've done for you," Bree said, her voice as cold as ice. "I made you popular. I got you a boyfriend. Don't you know I can take it all away like *that*?" She snapped her fingers.

Lexie found herself unconsciously leaning into Jake, away from Bree, and he put one arm around her in a protective way that she liked. Was this an act? Bree seemed genuinely mad. Maybe Sally really had been keeping it a secret from her. But then how did Bree know to show up there?

A suspicion struck her. Could Bree have weaseled the information out of Riley?

"Oh, for heaven's sake," Sally said. "Don't be a drama queen, Bree. I just wanted to go to the movies. You're not the be-all and end-all of my social life."

"You'll be lucky to *have* a social life after this," Bree said. "Ian, come with me." She turned regally, swinging her hair back from her forehead.

"Please," Sally scoffed. "He's my boyfriend."

"Not if I don't want him to be," Bree said. "Come along, Ian."

Ian hesitated, looking back and forth between

them. Sally's mouth dropped open. "For real?" she said. "Ian!"

"I can get you Amy Sorrento," Bree said to him.

"Okay," Ian said with a shrug. "Maybe she won't fuss at me like this one does."

Jake snorted.

"You kiss like a wet fish, anyway!" Sally called as Ian trailed after Bree. "Troglodyte!"

Jake and Lexie exchanged uncomfortable glances. Lexie wasn't sure what they were supposed to do. Sally wasn't exactly her friend, but they couldn't just walk away from her after that.

"Oh my God," Sally huffed, blowing strands of hair out of her face. "What a waste of three months *that* was. I'm sorry, you guys, we totally ruined your date."

"It's okay," Lexie said. *Especially since it's not even a real date.*

"I guess you guys should go to dinner without me," Sally said. "I'll just go home and start cutting Ian out of photographs or something."

"That sounds terrible, Sally," Lexie said. "You should come with us." Besides, she had no idea what she and Jake would talk about for an entire dinner by themselves. Would they still act like it was a date? As long as Sally was there, she could keep pretending it really was.

"Yeah," Jake said halfheartedly.

"Oh, sure," Sally said. "Third wheel on your one-week anniversary. I'm sure that's exactly what you want."

"We could call Colin," Lexie said. "I'm sure he'd be happy to come join us. And then you wouldn't feel like a third wheel."

Sally brightened a little. "Really? Wouldn't that be weird?"

"He won't mind," Lexie said. "Right, Jake?"

"Sure," Jake said. "I guess I can share you this once." He took her hand and squeezed it. She wondered what that meant.

Sally loaned Lexie her cell phone, and although he grumbled a bit in his Colin way about being in the middle of filming, he managed to make it to the diner in record time. He slid into the booth, next to Sally, before they'd even had a chance to order.

"Hey, Colin," Sally said. "Sorry to drag you out into the world on a Friday night. You'll never believe how I got ditched."

As she launched into the story of Ian and Bree,

Jake leaned sideways and tapped on the back of Lexie's hand. She jumped.

"Want to share fries?" he said.

"Sure, okay," Lexie answered. She thought it was interesting to watch Sally transform her whole three-month relationship with Ian into a funny story. It was as if Sally's life could be a TV show in her own mind — something hilarious that happened to someone else. The way she described it to Colin, it really did seem very funny. But Lexie couldn't imagine doing that herself. When Jake went off to date someone else, she wouldn't be able to tell sidesplitting stories about pretending to be his girlfriend. She would just be sad.

After dinner, they went back to Colin and Lexie's house and baked cookies, filming themselves with Colin's camera, until their mother finally announced that it was time for Sally and Jake to go home. Lexie realized that she hadn't been worrying about how to act on the date for at least a couple of hours. It had been like any other night when Jake came over, except that Sally was there, too.

And there was one other difference. Lexie walked Sally and Jake to the door, where Sally's mom was waiting outside in the car. Sally started down the porch steps, but Jake hesitated in the doorway.

Oh my God, Lexie thought. *It's the end of the date. Don't real couples kiss at the end of a date? Will Sally think it's weird if we don't? Does it matter, if she's not friends with Bree anymore?*

Jake looked into her eyes, and Lexie held her breath. On one hand, she wanted him to. Of course she wanted him to; she'd been wanting Jake to kiss her for almost three years. But if this was her first kiss . . . she wanted it to be real. She wanted it to be important to the guy as well as to her. She wanted Jake to kiss her because he wanted to, not because he was playing a role.

"Um, good night," she said quickly, stepping forward to hug him good-bye. Maybe that would let him know that he didn't have to do anything else.

His arms tightened around her and it seemed for a moment like time slowed down, and she could have stood there forever, pressed against him. She breathed in the smell of his hair and felt the warmth of his face right next to hers.

Finally he let go and stepped back, and she did, too, trying to act casual, like that had been a perfectly ordinary hug.

"Okay. Good night," he said. He ducked his head, kissed her quickly on the cheek, and then turned, jumping down the steps. Within moments, he had vanished into the night.

And that was the end of Lexie's first date.

chapter 8

Lexie spent most of Saturday in a hammock in her backyard, reading library books while Thorn snoozed on her stomach. Colin shut himself in his room and didn't come out until dinnertime, and then he wouldn't tell her what he'd been doing. *Fine, then,* Lexie thought. *You keep your secrets and I'll keep mine.*

Sunday morning at breakfast, her dad announced that he wanted them to wash the car. Colin groaned and smacked his head onto the table.

"Come on, champ," Mr. Willis said, clapping his son on the shoulder. "It'll be fun, right, Lexie? Oh, you guys might want to wear your bathing suits."

Lexie giggled. Last time they'd been given this chore, she and Colin had wound up wetter than the car in the end. He hated it, but she thought it was kind of fun. Especially when it was hot and sunny outside, like it was that day.

Her dad pulled the car out of the garage into the driveway and got buckets and sponges while Lexie and Colin changed. Lexie put on her black bathing suit with jean shorts and flip-flops and clipped her hair up out of the way with a large silver butterfly clip. When she went downstairs, her mother looked disappointed.

"I was hoping I'd finally get to see the bikini I bought you," Mrs. Willis said.

"Sorry, Mom," Lexie said, feeling guilty. "I figured since I'd be getting messy, this one was better." She hurried through the screen door before her mother could argue with her.

Colin was already inside the car, vacuuming between and under the seats. Lexie changed the pine-scented tree that hung in the front window, and then she wiped down all the hard surfaces. As soon as Colin was finished, she ran to get the hose.

"Stand back," she warned, and he jumped out of the way. Lexie turned on the hose, and her dog Alanna immediately came running over to throw herself under the spray.

"Alanna!" Lexie protested, trying to point the hose away. The pug woofed and chased the water across the driveway, running frantically around the car to get to it. Lexie started laughing, so she didn't see the person standing at the bottom of the driveway until she whirled around and sprayed water all over him.

"Hey!"

"Oops!" Lexie shut off the hose immediately, but it was too late. Riley was thoroughly drenched. And, as he had been the first time she'd seen him, he was wearing jeans and a long-sleeved shirt, which weren't likely to dry fast.

"Oh, no! I'm sorry!" Lexie cried. "I didn't see you there."

"Dude, you totally soaked me," Riley said. He didn't sound happy.

"Who's he?" Colin asked. Lexie shoved the hose into his hands.

"Wait here," she called to Riley. She ran inside, grabbed a towel from the linen closet, and ran back out. By then Riley had pulled off his dripping shirt and was wringing it out.

"Here," she said, handing him the towel. "I'm really sorry. What are you doing here?"

"I thought I'd stop by and say hey," Riley said, rubbing his hair with the towel. "I didn't know your driveway was a water hazard."

"How'd you know where I live?" she asked.

"It wasn't hard to figure out," he said. He kicked off his sneakers, pulled off his socks, and dried his feet.

"Who's this?" Colin said again, coming up behind Lexie.

"This is Riley," Lexie said. *You'd know all about him if you ever bothered to ask me how tennis camp was going.* "Riley, this is my twin brother, Colin."

"Twins," Riley said, nodding thoughtfully. "That's cool. You don't see a lot of girl-boy twins."

Ha! Lexie thought. *Wrong thing to say!*

"Are you kidding?" Colin said. "There are plenty. Alanis Morissette has a twin brother."

"Wade," Lexie supplied. She'd heard all this before.

"Giovanni Ribisi has a twin sister, and so does Kiefer Sutherland."

"Marissa and Rachel."

"And Scarlett Johansson has a twin brother."

"Hunter," Lexie said. "Aren't those the best names? Scarlett and Hunter. Much better than Alanis and Wade."

"Whoa, whoa," Riley said, waving his hands.

"I yield already! You win. I guess there are millions. I had no idea."

Colin looked smug. He liked showing off the stuff he knew.

"Here, if we put your shirt here, it'll dry faster," Lexie said. She took Riley's shirt from him and draped it over the porch railing, in the sun. He dropped his socks and sneakers on the step.

"So what are you doing?" he said. "Apart from soaking innocent bystanders?"

"We're washing the car," Lexie said.

"Want to help?" Colin offered.

"Colin!" Lexie said. "I'm *sure* Riley doesn't want to wash our car with us." And she wasn't sure she wanted him to stick around that long, especially shirtless. He kept giving her this slanty look and smile, like he thought she had deliberately gotten him to take his shirt off. As if! Sure, he was cute, but she'd seen him and Jake next to each other at the pool, and Jake was much cuter. In her opinion, anyway.

"I'd love to," Riley said. "Hand me that hose." He smirked.

"Don't even think about it," Lexie said, backing up. "Riley, don't you dare!" She ducked behind the car just as he grabbed the hose from Colin and turned it on her. He chased her around the car and she fled shrieking down the driveway, straight into Jake's arms.

"Whoa," he said, catching her elbows, and they were both caught in the spray as Riley deluged them.

Lexie shoved her wet hair back, laughing. Jake was looking over her shoulder at Riley, and he wasn't smiling.

"Oops," Riley said. "You caught us." He grinned and spread his arms like he was being held at gunpoint.

"Caught you doing what?" Jake asked. Lexie wondered the same thing. Why would Riley put it like that?

There was an awkward pause. Jake was still holding on to Lexie's elbows. Colin glanced at each of them, looking confused.

"I got Riley wet by accident," Lexie said. "He just stopped by, and he wanted to help wash the car . . . um . . ." Why did it suddenly sound lame and unbelievable?

"Yeah, man, sorry," Riley said. "We were just having fun. It's not what it looks like."

Not what it looks like? Lexie thought. *Doesn't it*

look like we're washing the car? There's nothing to feel weird about here. Right?

"What are you up to?" Lexie said, trying to sound casual, although it was difficult while Jake still had her pinned.

"Maybe I can stay and help, too," Jake said. "After all, now I'm as wet as you guys." He glanced down at Lexie and finally smiled. "Hey, girlfriend." He gave her a wet, squishy hug and she hid her smile in his chest.

"I saw Riley ride by in this direction," he whispered in her ear. "So I figured I'd come to make sure he wasn't bothering you. Hope that's okay."

"Of course," she said softly. "As long as you had a good, heroic reason for coming. We wouldn't want you to stop by just to say hi or anything crazy."

Jake winked at her and then slung his arm over her shoulder as they went back up the driveway. He and Riley exchanged dark glances as they passed, but Jake bent down and grabbed a sponge without commenting.

"Hey, Colin," he said. "I've been reading about *The Matrix* some more. Did you know that some of the scenes in the movie are based on scenes in Japanese anime movies? I think we're going to have to rent *Ghost in the Shell* and *Akira* to compare. Animefest, what do you think, Lexie?"

"Sure, sounds awesome," she said. He tossed her a sponge and then threw another one over to Riley, a little harder, so that soap bubbles spattered across Riley's chest.

"Come on, Riley," Jake said cheerfully. "Let's wash this car."

Between the four of them, it took almost no time at all. Lexie noticed that Riley was a lot more subdued now that Jake was there. He didn't try to spray her again, and he mostly acted like he really wanted to get out of there. But whenever he saw her looking at him, he'd give her that crooked smile, and he kept edging over to work closer to her.

"Oh my heavens," a voice said behind them. Lexie turned to find her parents standing on the porch. Mrs. Willis put her hands on her hips. "How did you all get so wet?"

"Serves me right for putting teenagers and a hose together on a hot day," Mr. Willis said with a grin.

"*I* didn't get wet," Colin pointed out in a superior voice.

"We could always fix that, you know," Lexie threatened.

"I think that is quite enough," Mrs. Willis said quickly.

"Yes, good work, kids," Lexie's dad said. "The car looks great."

"Jake, would you like to join us for cookies?" her mom added. "Freshly homemade!"

Riley popped out from behind the car and Lexie's mom jumped.

"Cookies?" Riley said. "Did someone say cookies?"

"Who is *this*?" Mr. Willis asked. Neither he nor Lexie's mom looked thrilled about having a strange, shirtless boy in their driveway.

"That's Riley," Lexie said. "He's in the tennis camp with us."

"Oh," Mrs. Willis said, mollified. "That's nice. Come on in."

Lexie was relieved to see Riley put his shirt back on before they all trooped into the house. He was sort of jumpy around her parents, like he wasn't sure what they would think of him, but he said all the right polite things about the cookies. He bolted out of his chair as soon as he was done.

"Well, I gotta run," he said. "See you tomorrow, Lexie."

"Yup, we'll see you tomorrow," Jake said,

scooting his chair next to Lexie's. Lexie risked a glance at her mother, who was washing dishes in the sink and pretending not to pay attention. Lexie was sure she spotted a tiny smile on her face.

"Bye, Riley," Lexie said.

The screen door banged behind him.

"Have I mentioned I really don't like that guy?" Jake said.

chapter 9

On Monday, Bree was leaning against the check-in booth as they came up the path from the parking lot. It was a horribly hot day; Lexie already felt tired and sweaty from the bike ride. But Bree looked cool and crisp, like a tall glass of evil lemonade. She was wearing her lacy bikini, with a white sarong looped around her waist and white slip-on sandals on her feet. Her sunglasses were giant and reflected the light in a metallic way, hiding her eyes. Even so, Lexie could feel them on her, a grim stare full of scheming and revenge plans, as she walked closer.

"Oh, hi, Lexie," Bree said with a sweet smile as they walked up. "Can I talk to you for a second — just us girls?" She wrapped her hands around Jake's upper arm and leaned playfully into him. "You don't mind if I steal your *girlfriend* for a minute, do you, Jakey?"

"Uh," Jake said. Lexie could tell he was as

confused as she was. Were they supposed to pretend the fight with Sally on Friday night hadn't happened?

"Just for a *minute*," Bree said, tousling his hair. "I'm sure you two can be apart for *one minute* without your cuteness dropping to dangerously low levels." She linked her arm through Lexie's. "We need some *girl time*."

Jake stepped forward as if to pull Lexie away, but Bree marched her off down the path toward the tennis courts too fast for either of them to object.

"Lexie," Bree whispered with fake enthusiasm. "I heard a rumor that Jake's *birthday* is this Wednesday! Oh my God! You must be so excited. What a great opportunity to show what a terrific girlfriend you are, right? I'm sure you have something really amazing planned, don't you?"

Lexie's heart sank. She had managed not to think about it all weekend, but now Jake's birthday was only two days away, and she still didn't have a present for him. Bree had zeroed in on her biggest worry.

"Um," she said, "well, I —"

"I just wanted you to know," Bree said, "that I am here to help. I love party planning and I am *so*

116

good at it. I mean, you *are* throwing him a party, right? Guys love parties, especially surprise parties! Is it going to be at your house? Because if you want, we could have it at my house. My house is enormous and my parents are never home so they won't care."

"Oh, I don't —" Lexie started.

"We have a ton of food, so don't worry about that. And I can take care of inviting everyone. I'll make sure it's the *right* guest list. All you have to do is find a way to get him to my house. You're clever; you'll think of something." Bree shook her hair back from her face and smiled, the sunlight glinting off her sunglasses. "And buy him a perfect present, of course. But I'm sure you already have that covered."

"But wait," Lexie said, "what if — I don't think he —"

"Wednesday, six o'clock," Bree said brightly. "Everyone will be there, so don't forget. It's going to be a *great* party. He'll feel so lucky to have you for his girlfriend." She patted Lexie once on the head and then turned and swept back down the path. Sally passed her on the way, but Bree tilted her nose up and looked away as if Sally were too insignificant to notice.

"What was that all about?" Sally asked, coming up to Lexie. "Are you okay? You look kind of pale."

"Can I borrow your cell phone?" Lexie asked.

"Sure." Sally fished it out of her bag and Lexie dialed her home number quickly.

Her mom answered. "Hello?"

"Hey, Mom. Can I talk to Colin?"

"He's not here, dear. What's wrong?"

"He's not *there*? Where is he?" Lexie was puzzled. Colin never got up that early on his own, and as far as she knew, he didn't have anywhere to go. She wondered if this had anything to do with whatever he'd been hiding from her the other day.

"I can tell him you called," Mrs. Willis said. "But maybe I can help with something?"

"No, that's okay," Lexie said. "I'll talk to him when I get home. Bye, Mom."

Her mom sighed. "Bye, Lexie."

Lexie handed the phone back to Sally. How could Colin not be there? She needed his advice so badly. Or Karina's. That was who Lexie really wanted to talk to — a girl who understood how complicated this was. What was Lexie supposed to do now? She didn't want to lure Jake to Bree's for a surprise party. But if they didn't show up, it would be weird and embarrassing. And she had to come up with an idea for a present — an idea that said "girlfriend," not "best friend's sister."

"Come on," Sally said, slipping the phone into her bag. "Tell me all about it as we walk. What's Bree done now?"

Lexie found herself explaining Bree's whole party scheme. By the time they reached the tennis courts, Sally was shaking her head.

"That is so typical of Bree," she said. "She thinks she's being generous, but she just ends up being controlling and scary." Lexie somehow doubted that Bree was trying to be generous with this plan, but she didn't say anything. Sally and Bree might still make up and be friends again, after all.

"And don't even try to tell her you want to do things your own way," Sally continued. "She can't comprehend people disagreeing with her." Sally put down her tennis racket and pulled her hair back into a ponytail. "I don't know, Lexie, you might have to go."

"Seriously?" Lexie said. Somehow she'd expected Sally to tell her not to go.

"Well, unless you want to tell her yourself that you don't want to," Sally said. "Or just let her plan it and not show up, which would be kind of rough. But listen, it won't be that bad. Her parties always have great food and they have Ping-Pong and foosball in the basement. You could show up for a couple of hours and then take Jake out for ice cream afterward, just the two of you."

Lexie felt ill. That sounded like some serious concentrated Bree time, which meant a ton of opportunities for Bree to do something mean to her.

"Don't worry," Sally said. "Bree's crazy, but she's not evil."

I'm not so sure about that, Lexie thought.

"Hey," Riley said, slouching up to them. "I had fun on Sunday," he said to Lexie.

Sally raised her eyebrows.

"Washing my parents' car," Lexie said quickly. "With Jake and Colin."

"Yeah, too bad," Riley said. "We might have had more fun just the two of us." He gave her arm a quick squeeze and then meandered away.

"What a flirt," Sally whispered. When Lexie's eyes widened, she added, "I mean him, not you. Like, she's taken, pal, back off. Right?"

Lexie rubbed her arm and stared at Riley's retreating back. Did he really like her *that* way?

He seemed to . . . but why? He thought she was with Jake, so he shouldn't be flirting with her. It was all very confusing.

That afternoon they began the water volleyball tournament that Cynthia had been talking about. Lexie's team won their game, which made Jake splash around triumphantly in a totally adorable way.

As he dropped her off at home, Jake said, "Hey, Lexie, ask Colin about watching those anime movies this weekend, okay?"

"Sure," she said. She watched him pedal away, waving when he looked back right before turning off onto his street.

To her surprise, Alanna and Thorn were on the porch. Their leashes were tied to the railing, and their squashed little faces were pressed against the screen door as if they'd been yearning to go back inside for days and days.

"Hey, guys," Lexie said, crouching down and unclipping them. "What are you doing out here?" She scratched behind their ears and they both tried to climb on her knees to snuffle at her face.

The instant she swung the door open, both pugs bolted toward the living room. There was a yelp and then a thud. Lexie ran after them and found her mom in a contorted position on the carpet with the dogs clambering all over her.

"Mom?" she gasped. "Are you okay?"

"Yes, yes," Mrs. Willis said, untangling herself. She reached for the remote and paused the DVD. Lexie realized that the people on-screen were all in leotards and were now frozen in the same weird position.

"What are you doing?" Lexie asked.

"I'm *trying* to do yoga," her mother said. "But certain *dogs* were making it *very difficult.*" Alanna snorted and wagged her tail triumphantly.

"Yoga?" Lexie said, dropping her bag inside the door. "I thought you went to a class for that."

"Well, I got this DVD, so I thought I'd try it. It's very good if you can get through it without having your face licked off." Her mom gave Thorn a stern look, but the pug just sat there with a goofy expression.

"Can I watch?" Lexie said. "Maybe I can distract the dogs."

"Of course," her mother said delightedly. "You can even join me if you like. I just started."

"Um . . . okay," Lexie said. She had to admit she was curious. She sat down on the carpet next to her mother as Mrs. Willis skipped back to the beginning of the DVD.

"So how was tennis today?" Mrs. Willis asked.

"The same," Lexie said. She imitated her mother's cross-legged position, trying to sit up tall and keep her back straight. The woman on the TV was yammering about breathing.

"Anything exciting happening?"

Lexie debated with herself for a minute and then decided to share a small part of her problem with her mom.

"It's Jake's birthday on Wednesday," Lexie said, "and I have to get him a present."

"Ah." Her mother shook her head. "I made the same mistake with your father."

"Mistake?" Lexie repeated.

"Starting to date him right before his birthday. Trying to come up with the perfect gift when you barely know a guy — it's terrible!"

"I wouldn't say I 'barely know' Jake," Lexie pointed out.

"Of course, dear. And he must be easier to shop for than your dad. I can't even get that man a tie without earning a lecture on appropriate colors for the office."

"Well, *I* thought the orange was cool," Lexie said loyally. Dad had had to buy all his own ties since that Christmas.

"Think about what Jake likes," Mrs. Willis said, "and what he's interested in. Something personal is always better than something expensive."

Then they had to stop talking because the woman on-screen was explaining a position called the "downward dog," which, as far as Lexie could tell, was named that because it brought her mom's face down close to the floor, where Thorn and Alanna could easily lick it.

She thought about what her mother had said. What did Jake like?

If only the answer was me . . .

♥ chapter 10

Bree wasn't taking any chances. At lunch on Wednesday, she sat down across from Lexie and Jake, even though Sally was on the other side of Lexie. Sally and Lexie exchanged glances. Bree hadn't spoken to Sally since the incident at the movies, but Sally still seemed to think they'd make up soon. Lexie wasn't sure where she'd gotten that idea, since Lexie had never seen Bree forgive anyone, but Sally kept cheerfully saying, "Oh, Bree will come around."

"Sally's an optimist," Colin had said when Lexie had told him about that. "She can't tell when people are genuinely evil because she's too nice to be evil herself. That's exactly the kind of person the genuinely evil types like the best."

"What on earth are you talking about?" Lexie had answered.

"It's in plenty of movies," Colin said with a

shrug, keeping his eyes on their video game. "Sally's like Queen Amidala in *Star Wars*. She couldn't tell Anakin was going evil until it was too late, because she was too good a person herself."

"Queen Amidala?" Lexie said. "Sally has way better fashion sense than her."

But perhaps Colin was right about Sally's people sense. When Bree sat down, Sally said, "Hey, Bree, how's it going?" and held out her bag of Mini Oreos. "Want one?"

Bree ignored her.

"Where's Riley?" she asked Lexie.

"I'm not sure," Lexie said, glancing at Sally.

"Oh," Bree said. "I thought you might know."

Why? Lexie wondered. "Mr. Giambi probably kept him to help find the tennis balls he knocked into the bushes," she said. "He seemed kind of mad about that."

"Oh, Lexie, dear," Bree said, all sugary and fake. "That reminds me. Don't forget to come by and borrow that book tonight." She winked in a really obvious way. "I should be home by *six*. So *don't forget*. It's very important."

"What book?" Jake asked. Lexie could understand his confusion. For one, why would Bree be lending Lexie a book? Why would Bree even own a book?

"Um," she said. Bree narrowed her eyes and smiled at Lexie, leaving her to flounder through a lame explanation. "Um," Lexie said again. "It's — it's about volleyball, water volleyball, you know, for the tournament."

Sally choked on her soda and got up quickly. Lexie could see her shoulders shaking with laughter as she hurried off to the bathroom.

"They have books about pool volleyball?" Jake said skeptically.

"They do," Bree said, "and Lexie is going to borrow mine."

"Okaaaay," Jake said. "Anything to give us a competitive edge. We're going to win this thing, right, Lexie?"

"Absolutely," she said, and he stole a carrot stick from her, grinning.

Lexie glanced across the table at Bree, but the blond girl was delicately crunching a piece of celery and didn't look like she was going anywhere. And really, the whole point of Lexie's present for Jake was to prove her girlfriend status to Bree, so she might as well give it to him in front of her, no matter how awkward it made her feel.

"Here," she said, pulling a wrapped gift out of her shoulder bag and handing it to Jake. "Happy birthday!"

Jake looked surprised. "But —"

"I know we haven't been dating long," Lexie said, trying to communicate, *Shut up and open it*, with her eyes. "But hopefully you'll like it."

They'd already had a mini-birthday breakfast that morning, at Lexie's house. Her mom had made banana pancakes for her and Jake and Colin and they'd stuck a candle in one and all sung "Happy Birthday" completely off-key. Jake had probably thought that was the extent of his birthday celebrations. Boy, was he going to be surprised.

"Wow, thanks," he said, pulling off the ribbon. "You didn't have to do this."

"Of course she did," Bree interjected. "She's your *girlfriend*, Jakey."

"Yeah," Lexie said. "Exactly."

"Oh," he said. "Ah." Then, as he ripped off the wrapping paper: "Wait, is this . . . Tupperware?"

"Cool, right?" Lexie said. "You can put food inside it, and it'll stay fresh. Isn't that a great idea? And look, the container is purple."

Jake gave her a puzzled look and she shook her head at him, laughing. "No, I didn't give you Tupperware for your birthday. Open the container, doofus."

He peeled back the plastic lid, and his face lit up exactly the way Lexie had been hoping it would.

Inside, nestled in rows across the bottom, were eighteen small chocolate cupcakes. On the top of each one, Lexie had written a letter in white chocolate frosting, so they spelled out HAPPY BIRTHDAY JAKE!

"Oh my God," he said. "Lexie, this is amazing. It's much too cool to eat."

"I hope not, because I'm planning to help you eat them," Lexie said.

"What?" Bree said impatiently. "Let me see."

Jake tilted the container toward her so she could see the cupcake message. He had a cute triumphant-looking smile on his face. Lexie guessed that she had played her part perfectly.

"Cupcakes?" Bree said. "How . . . sweet. What a clever way to save money, Lexie. I'm sure Jake appreciates your . . . thriftiness."

"It's the best present I've ever gotten," Jake

said, seeing Lexie start to deflate. He took the first mini cupcake out, peeled away the cup, and bit off half of it. Then he held out the other half to Lexie.

"Thanks," she said, turning pink. He batted her hand away and made her open her mouth so he could pop it in.

Colin and Sally had helped her bake them, with her mom supervising. Lexie suspected more chocolate had gone into Colin and Sally than into the cupcakes, but at least they'd ended up with eighteen good enough to give to Jake.

"So what else did you get him?" Bree asked. "Anything . . . lasting?" Her expression seemed to be saying, *Or is your relationship going to be as short-lived as these cupcakes?*

"I hope you didn't get me anything else," Jake said. "This is perfect enough for me."

The truth was Lexie did have another present for him in her pocket. But she was less sure about that one. She'd bought it a while before because it had made her think of him when she'd seen it, but she'd never found the opportunity to give it to him. But then, the day before, she'd shown it to Sally, who was convinced that he would love it. If he didn't, there was no way for Lexie to get it back. And she kind of liked hiding it in her shoe box, next to the origami whale.

"I — I thought I'd give it to him later," Lexie said.

"Oh, in *private*?" Bree said snidely.

Lexie nodded.

"Uh-huh," Bree said. "I'm sure." She clearly didn't believe that Lexie had anything else, but Lexie didn't want to prove it badly enough to give Jake this present in front of her.

"Well," Bree said, collecting her lunch remains, "you can tell me what it is later, Jakey. See you at six, Lexie, dear — oh, and try to be punctual, will you?"

She swept off, evidently feeling that she'd seen enough. Lexie felt sick just thinking about the evening. Who would Bree have invited? How would Jake react? He didn't love big gatherings of people any more than she did, although he was better at navigating through them. She wished there were a way to get out of it, but she hated the idea of a bunch of people standing around Bree's house wondering where they were and blaming Lexie for ruining the party.

"You don't have to give me anything else," Jake

said seriously, taking her hand. "I really love the cupcakes."

"And Bree was convinced, don't you think?" Lexie said. "That was girlfriendy of me, wasn't it?"

Jake looked down at their hands. "Yeah, it was," he said. "Good job. You, uh, nearly had me fooled, too."

"I do have something else," Lexie said. "But it might be kind of stupid. I don't know if you'll want it. If you don't want it, just give it back to me."

Jake grinned. "I'm sure if you picked it, it's awesome."

Hesitantly, she pulled a small cloth bag out of her shorts pocket and placed it in his hand. He untied the strings and poured out the contents onto the lunch table. A leather cord slithered out, and the small white whale strung on it made a clicking noise against the wood.

Jake touched the little whale, his smile growing. Lexie thought it was made of whalebone or shell; anyway, it felt smooth and was polished to a shine. Its little tail was lifted in a happy way, and tiny flippers were carved in the side.

"It's a necklace," Lexie said, "but it's supposed

to be a guy necklace. That's what the salesperson told me. But you don't have to wear it; I know it's weird to get a guy jewelry. I thought Bree might make fun of me if I gave it to you in front of her. But it made me think of you, because of the origami whales, but if you don't like it I can totally take it back —"

"Lexie, I love it," he said, interrupting her babbling. "Will you put it on me?"

She blinked at him as he lifted the leather cord around his neck. "Really?"

"Yeah, of course," he said. "I want to show off my girlfriend's awesome taste."

He scooted around with his back to her, so he didn't see her face as she took the ends of the cord. She felt so strange, finally giving this to him. What if he thought it was just a pretend present? What if he had no idea that it actually meant something to her? How could he know? She had always imagined giving this to him and telling him at the same time that she'd liked him for ages, and that she'd been saving the necklace all that time. But she obviously couldn't tell him that now. He thought they were only pretending.

She tied the ends of the cord in a knot, carefully keeping a finger between the knot and his skin so she wouldn't catch any of the soft golden-brown hairs on the back of his neck.

It looked perfect on him. The whale hung just below the hollow of his throat, and it didn't look girly at all, which Lexie had worried about. Jake just looked even more handsome, like he'd walked straight out of some CW beach show.

"Thanks, Lexie," he said, wrapping his arms around her and pulling her in for a hug. She rested her head on his shoulder and felt the muscles of his back below her palms. "This is the greatest birthday," Jake said.

I hope you still think so after tonight, Lexie thought.

chapter 11

"Have I mentioned that I don't get this?" Jake said as they parked their bikes at the bottom of Bree's long driveway. "Tell me again why you're borrowing a book from Bree?"

Lexie shrugged. "It seemed easier than saying no to her." Well, that part was true. Luckily, Jake had insisted on coming with her; he didn't want to leave her alone with Bree, which she appreciated.

"I guess," Jake said. "Man, her house is huge."

They locked their bikes to the fence beside the driveway. The path up to Bree's front door was made of neat zigzagging bricks and wound around several flower beds before reaching the tall marble columns and gigantic gilt-encrusted doorway.

"Isn't this a little weird?" Jake whispered to Lexie as they followed the path. "Like they're forcing their guests to take the scenic route and admire the flowers? What if you just want to get to the door already?"

"Maybe it's a test to make sure that you *really* want to get there," Lexie joked.

"I'm guessing they don't have many visitors, then," Jake said with a smile.

Lexie rang the doorbell. There was a long pause, and then the curtain beside the door was whisked aside and a nervous female face — red-haired, big-nosed — peeked out before getting yanked back.

Another pause. The door opened.

The redhead was standing there bobbing and bowing, looking terrified. She was wearing a shapeless maid's uniform and an apron that she kept twisting in her hands.

"Oh, get out of the way, Greta," Bree snapped, popping out from behind the door. "How hard is it to let a guest in? I mean, seriously. *Hello*, Jake!"

"Hey," he said, taking Lexie's hand.

Lexie felt instantly awkward, as she was sure Bree had intended. Lexie was still wearing her bathing suit from earlier that day, with a white T-shirt and red shorts over it. Bree, on the other hand, was wearing a sleeveless, formfitting white sheath dress that had side slits all the way up her legs and an oval cutout from her neck nearly half-way down her chest. Her shoes were very high white espadrilles. She looked like she'd just stepped out of a movie. Lexie glanced down at her sneakers, embarrassed.

"Come on back to the pool," Bree said. She pushed her sleek blond hair back and waved her hand, leading the way through the cavernous house.

"I guess her obsessions are genetic," Jake whispered to Lexie. The whole house was white — white leather couches, white marble staircases, white silk lampshades, white bearskin rugs. The only art on the walls were large black-and-white photographs of Bree, her older sister, and her parents, all in perfect frozen poses with perfect frozen smiles. Lexie got the impression that if she touched anything, she'd either break it or leave dirty fingerprints all over it.

Bree flung open the double doors to the patio, whirled around, and cried, "Surprise!"

"*Surprise!*" yelled the crowd of people gathered outside. There were about thirty people scattered around the pool. Lexie recognized most of them from school, but she wasn't sure she'd ever spoken to half of them. She wondered if Jake had.

Jake's mouth dropped open.

"Happy birthday, Jakey," Bree cooed. She wrapped her hands around his arm and tugged him away from Lexie. "Come on, say hello to everyone. They're here to celebrate you! Lexie can have you back later."

Jake gave Lexie a baffled look and she spread her hands helplessly. "It was Bree's idea," she said.

"Of course it was," Bree said. "I just *love* throwing parties. And Lexie didn't have any idea what to do, so I thought I should help." She dragged Jake down the patio steps to the edge of the pool, where a group of sporty types started slapping him on the back and offering him drinks.

Lexie glanced around and, to her relief, spotted Colin off by himself on a lounge chair.

"Thank God you're here," she said, sitting on the edge of the chair next to him.

"I can't believe you talked me into this," he muttered, poking the ice in his glass with a small pink umbrella.

"Hey, this is all your fault, Mr. Bright Ideas," Lexie said. "You're the reason Bree is out to get me, so the least you can do is show up to one party."

"You should have seen the look on her face,"

he said with a grin. "When she opened the door and saw me there — I seriously thought she was going to pretend I was invisible and just slam it shut again. But I was like, 'Hey, Bree, thanks for throwing the cool party,' and walked right in."

"You didn't!" Lexie said, impressed.

"I did. She kind of harrumphed and waved in this direction. So I came out, got a soda, and I've been sitting right here ever since."

"Do we know anyone else here?" Lexie asked, drawing her legs up on the chaise longue.

"Depends on your definition of 'know,'" Colin said. "For instance, Amy Sorrento is here."

Lexie felt a twinge of jealousy. Jake had dated Amy for four months. She was part Latina, part ballerina, and all gorgeous but way too demanding, snobby, and cold for Jake. Lexie had never understood why he'd liked her in the first place.

"Really?" she said. "Is she dating Ian, like Bree promised?"

"I haven't seen him," Colin said, shaking his head.

Amy passed them just then, but she didn't bother to glance down and acknowledge their presence. She patted her smooth bun of glossy brown hair and sailed over to Jake, greeting him with a large smile as if she hadn't dumped him only a couple of months earlier.

"I hate parties," Colin said.

"I just hate these kinds of parties," Lexie said. "Stand, hold a drink, smile painfully, look interested in boring chitchat, comment on the weather, avoid the subject of school, wish desperately that there were any good movies to talk about, shift drink to other hand, wonder how many peanuts one can eat without looking like a ravenous hippo, nod politely, stand some more."

"Speaking of peanuts," Colin said, "check out the table behind us."

Lexie swiveled around and discovered a low plastic table (white, of course) with three trays of appetizers on it.

"Wow, excellent location-scouting, Colin," she said, snagging a pastry ball that turned out to have sausage in the middle.

"I thought so," he said with a modest nod.

After about twenty minutes, Jake finally managed to fight his way over to them.

"I can't believe you abandoned me like that," he said, flopping down on the ground next to Lexie. He leaned back against her legs. "Do you know how many times I've had to say, 'Yeah, it *has* been hot this summer, hasn't it?' in the last ten minutes?"

"This'll make you feel better," Lexie said, handing him a crab dumpling.

"Thanks," he said. "And thanks for the party."

"It really wasn't my idea," she said. "I'm sorry for letting you be surprised."

"It's okay," he said. "I've never been to a Bree McKennis party, but I guess people weren't exaggerating about the food. What are those?"

"Something involving cheese," Lexie said, passing him the tray.

"Awesome," he said. "If you can make it to the other side of the pool, there are mini hamburgers and tiny French fries to match."

"Just think," Colin said, "if you dated Bree, all this could be yours."

Which is exactly the point of all this, I'm sure, Lexie thought. How could she compete with flawless beauty, impeccable fashion sense, and a house like this? Her little cupcakes didn't begin to compare.

"Yeah," Jake said, "but then I'd have to date Bree."

As if on cue, Bree swayed her way through the

crowd and dropped a large box in Jake's lap. "Jake, darling, here's your birthday present," she purred.

"Oh," he said. "You didn't really —"

"Of course I did!" She crouched beside him, revealing a long slim line of her leg. "Open it at once."

With the expression of a guy who was pretty sure his present was about to explode, Jake hesitantly peeled the glittering gold-and-white wrapping paper off and opened the box.

"Whoa," he said. "Seriously?"

Nestled in the thin folds of crepe paper was a black leather jacket.

"Happy birthday, Jake," Bree said with a triumphant smile. "It's all the way from Italy. And very expensive."

"I'll bet," Jake said. Lexie could tell he was feeling uncomfortable. She wasn't exactly thrilled herself. It would take her several lifetimes to babysit up enough money for a present like that.

"How did you get him a present from Italy?" Colin asked curiously.

Bree gave him a disdainful look. "We had it in our emergency gift drawer. I think it'll fit you perfectly, Jake, dear. Let's go find a mirror and try it on! Come on, come on." She grabbed his hand

and pulled. With a sigh, he climbed to his feet and followed her.

"Jake, darling," Colin said, imitating her, "come into my lair and let me tie you up."

Lexie saw a blur of motion out of the corner of her eye, but before she could react, a pair of male arms had seized her and swung her up off her feet.

"Put me down!" she protested, shoving Riley's shoulders. He tightened his grip on her and gave her his sly smile.

"Feel like going swimming?" he said.

"No," she said. "Do *not* throw me in the pool, Riley."

"But don't you want to cool off?" he said, swinging her dangerously close to the edge. "I think I owe you a soaking."

"You do not!" she said, struggling to get down. "We're totally even! Riley!"

"She doesn't want to get wet, man," Colin said.

"What do you know about it?" Riley said, but he put her down. She stepped out of arm's reach quickly. "Aw, I'm just kidding around, Lexie."

"Well, it wouldn't be funny," she said. Yes, he was kind of joking, but she was sure he would happily have dumped her into the pool without even thinking about the fact that she didn't have a change of clothes or that she'd look like an idiot in front of everyone. A wet idiot.

"Have you seen the basement?" Riley asked cheerfully. "It's totally awesome."

"Not yet," Lexie said.

"I'll show you," he said, taking her elbow. "There's foosball and Ping-Pong and air hockey and Ms. Pac-Man and pinball —"

"Colin, don't you want to come?" Lexie said, seeing that her brother wasn't standing to follow them.

"I'm going to get one of those hamburgers first," Colin said, apparently missing the significance of her look. Lexie sighed inwardly. Sally would have understood! "I'll find you in a minute."

"Okay. Bring me one, too," she said. "Soon." Riley gave her a weird look and she added, "I mean, because I'm starving — you know, totally starving."

"Sure," Colin said.

Lexie reluctantly followed Riley down a few steps to a lower patio paved with sparkling gray stone. A set of glass doors led into the basement, which, to her dismay, was empty. She'd expected to find other partygoers in there playing with the games.

"Isn't it cool?" Riley said, wandering over to the foosball table. He spun a row of players around and then looked up and grinned at her. "Want to play?"

Lexie felt bad. Riley hadn't been anything but nice to her. Why did she keep feeling uncomfortable around him? Was it because he seemed to like her? Or could it be because she liked him? She tried poking that thought, but her feelings for Riley still weren't anything like her feelings for Jake. Still, here was a cute guy flirting with her. She could at least be nice back.

"Okay, sure," she said, going around to the other side of the table. Riley fished a ball out of the side pocket and dropped it in.

Lexie wasn't really good at foosball, but Riley was hilariously bad. He basically played by spinning the players around and around as fast as he could. She couldn't help laughing at him, but luckily he didn't get offended.

She was winning 8–4 when a phone rang somewhere in the far corner of the room. Riley spun his players one more time and then announced, "I'm bored. Let's check out Ms. Pac-Man."

"Oh, okay," Lexie said. She followed him over to the arcade game, which had a place of honor in the center of the room, its back against a column. Just as she got up behind him, he turned and caught her wrists in his hands.

"Lexie," he said, "why don't you like me?"

She had been about to pull away, but when he said that, she stopped, feeling guilty again.

"What do you mean?" she said. "I do like you."

"But only as a friend — right?"

"Well," she said awkwardly, "Riley, I'm — I'm dating Jake." *Not to mention I'm secretly on a quest to convince him he's my soul mate.*

"Forget Jake," Riley said. "What if he weren't in the picture? Huh? What if you'd met me first?"

"I don't know," Lexie said. "I mean, I didn't, so — and Jake is — I'm sorry, Riley, but —"

Suddenly the door from the patio opened. Riley dropped her hands like lit firecrackers and sprang away from her as if he'd just been caught stealing diamonds.

It was Jake . . . and Amy Sorrento.

♥ chapter 12

"Jake!" Lexie said.

"Oh, man," Riley said. "We're so busted."

"What — no!" Lexie said. "What are you talk-ing about?"

Jake hesitated inside the doorway, looking con-fused. Amy still had one hand on the doorknob, and the other was resting lightly on Jake's shoul-der as if she owned him — as if he were her car, or her horse, or her umbrella stand.

"I guess we're not going to get any privacy in here, Jake," Amy said in a murmur that Lexie could clearly hear.

Lexie felt her heart sink. Jake and Amy had been looking for privacy? Why? Did she want him back? More importantly . . . did he want her back?

She couldn't really blame him. A real girlfriend sounded much better than a pretend girlfriend who he didn't want to date at all, even if that real girl-friend was an ice queen like Amy.

What was he thinking right then? Was he disappointed that they were interrupted? And did he really think she and Riley . . . ?

She couldn't tell from his expression, although she thought maybe he looked a little bit mad.

There was a tense pause, and then Jake seemed to take a breath and come back to the room, blinking. He gave his shoulders a small shake that dislodged Amy's hand, and he stepped across the space to Lexie.

"Hey," he said, and his smile made the knot of worry in her stomach melt away.

"Hey," she said, smiling back at him. He took her hand and turned to Amy.

"Amy, you remember Lexie," he said. Amy lifted her nose and looked down it at Lexie. She seemed even taller than Lexie remembered, and she was also dressed elegantly, in skinny jeans, a long purple top, and a sleek silver belt. Jake had tried to bring her out with Lexie and Colin a couple of times, but that had been a disaster. Amy clearly had no interest in talking to either of them, whereas Jake seemed more interested in their conversation than hers. That was close to the end of their relationship.

"Yeeees. Bree told me you were dating . . . her," Amy said. "Is it true?"

No, Lexie thought sadly. *It's not true. If it were, this would be the best moment ever, you skinny witch.*

"Yup," Jake said with no hesitation. "Lexie is my girlfriend." He shot a glare at Riley, as if that was a reminder for him, too.

"That's right," Lexie said. "He's with me." She couldn't resist giving Amy an enormous smile — a smile that said, *That's right, you lost him and now he's mine.*

Still, Lexie wondered if Jake felt as confident as he looked. The whole scheme had been for Bree's benefit, to protect him at summer camp. He probably hadn't expected the entire school to find out. Now everyone, including Amy and whatever girl he'd like next, really would think he'd dated her. Was he embarrassed about that?

The patio door opened and Bree came in, followed by a handful of other people. One of them was Colin, who wandered over to Lexie with a plate full of mini food.

"It's about time you showed up," she hissed.

"Believe it or not, someone actually spoke to

149

me," he said. "I wish I could tell you who, but it wasn't that memorable a conversation."

"Oh, *there* you are, Jake," Bree said. "I saw Amy whisking you away and I was like, 'Oh, no, we're not going to see *them* again for the rest of the night!'" She gave Lexie a sly look.

"We just couldn't resist the air-conditioning," Jake said.

"Me, too," Bree chirped. "Hey, who wants to play Truth or Dare?"

There was a chorus of "ooh, me!"s.

"Truth or Dare?" Jake said skeptically. "That's a little childish, don't you think?"

"Not if you play it right," Bree said with a coquettish smile. She plopped herself down on one of the fluffy white couches. "Come sit here with me, birthday boy." She patted the cushion next to her.

Jake glanced at Lexie. "We can go back outside," he said in a low voice.

"Wait, I want to play," Colin interjected in a whisper. "I've never been to a party with Truth or Dare before."

"I don't think you want to play Bree's version," Lexie said softly to him.

"Come on, guys," Colin said. "Just for a minute? Please?"

"It's up to you, Lexie," Jake said. "Whatever you decide."

"Um — okay," Lexie said. "Maybe it'll be fun." *Doubtful . . . but if it cheers Colin up, it might be worth it.*

Amy and Riley were already settling onto beanbags on the floor, and other people had taken the other couches and chairs. Bree patted the cushion beside her again, batting her eyelashes at Jake.

"Scoot over," Jake said to her firmly, holding Lexie's hand.

Bree sighed huffily and slid to the side so Jake and Lexie could both sit down. Colin dropped to the carpet at their feet.

"All right, I'll go first," Bree said. "Amy, truth or dare?"

Lexie breathed a quiet sigh of relief. She'd been sure Bree would go after her first.

"Dare," Amy said.

"Okay," Bree said. "I dare you to take off your shirt."

Before Lexie could blink, Amy had unclipped

her belt and pulled off the purple top. Underneath she was wearing a pink polka-dot bikini top.

"No fair!" Bree protested. "You're wearing your bathing suit!"

"As if I would have taken off my top otherwise!" Amy said in a mockingly scandalized tone. "Okay, my turn. Jake."

Lexie's heart sank. Would she make him kiss Bree? Or her? She didn't want her first kiss with Jake to be on a dare in front of all these people.

"Truth," Jake said.

Also dangerous, Lexie thought. *Considering how much truth we're hiding here.*

"Truth," Amy said slowly. "All right. Of all the girls in this room, who do you think is the prettiest? Be honest."

She and Bree both looked expectant. Of the two of them, Lexie would probably say Amy, because Bree's prettiness was harder around the edges, and Amy had really long eyelashes. But of all the girls in the room, Lexie would actually pick the redheaded girl on the sofa opposite her. Not only was she pretty but she also looked nice instead of scary. Lexie thought her name might be Clara, and she might be on the field hockey team —

"Lexie," Jake said. "Of course."

"Of course!" Bree parroted in an offended tone. "You don't have to say that just because she's your girlfriend. You're supposed to answer *truthfully*, Jake. I'm sure Lexie wouldn't want you to *lie*."

"I'm not lying," Jake said, putting his arm around Lexie's shoulders. "I'd think she was the prettiest even if she weren't my girlfriend. I love how long and curly Lexie's hair is, and she has beautiful brown eyes, and the cutest nose, and just a sprinkling of freckles, and the best smile —"

"Gag me with an artificial sweetener already," Bree said, rolling her eyes. Lexie was sure she'd turned a brilliant shade of red, but she kept her head resting on Jake's shoulder so she wouldn't have to meet anyone's eyes. Bree waved her hands. "Fine, whatever, blah blah blah, move on. Your turn."

"Okay," Jake said. "Colin."

Colin looked pleased. He thought seriously for a moment and then said, "Dare."

"Hmmm," Jake said. "Let's see. I dare you to . . ." He looked around the room thoughtfully and pointed. "I dare you to kiss Claire."

The redheaded field hockey player turned pink. *Clara, Claire, I was close,* Lexie thought.

Colin stood up awkwardly and so did Claire. He stepped over the rug and leaned forward; she leaned forward, too, and they ended up bumping lips more than kissing. Still, Lexie could tell that Colin was trying not to smile when he sat back down. She realized that Jake had done him a favor, especially by picking the nicest girl in the room. Amy or Bree might have refused to kiss him, which would have been terrible.

"Colin, it's your turn to ask someone," Lexie said, poking his shoulder.

"Right, okay," he said. "Uh —"

"And don't pick your sister," Bree said snidely. "Act like you actually know anybody else for once."

Colin flushed. "Bree," he said.

"Dare," she said promptly.

"Um." Colin picked at the carpet. "I dare you to tell us who the hottest guy in the room is."

"That's just a truth dressed up as a dare," Bree complained.

"That's my dare," Colin said stubbornly.

"Fine," Bree said. "I pick Riley. Now it's my turn. Lexie, darling, truth or dare?"

Riley was grinning. He looked for the first time

like he'd noticed that Bree was interested in him. Lexie was surprised Bree hadn't picked Jake as the hottest guy, but she wasn't surprised that she was the next to go. She had a feeling that that was what this had all been leading up to. "Um, truth," she said. She did not want to do anything Bree might dare her to do.

"Figures," Bree said, rolling her eyes again. "Okay, let me think." She tapped her chin with a manicured fingernail. "Lexie, Lexie. All right, tell us the truth." She leaned forward. "How long have you been in love with Jake?"

Cold prickles ran down Lexie's spine. Now what? Should she lie and say it had only been a couple of weeks? Should she tell the truth and admit that it had been years? Would Jake figure she was lying no matter what she said? Or would her voice give her away?

"Go on, Lexie, tell us," Bree said.

Lexie's eyes went to Amy, who was pretending to look bored. Would it be embarrassing to admit that she'd liked him while he had been dating Amy? She tipped her head back and looked at Jake.

His smoky-gray eyes were watching her. He

leaned his head against hers and whispered, "Don't worry."

Whatever that meant, it decided her. She would tell the truth.

"As long as I've known him," she said, lowering her gaze to meet Bree's.

She felt his arm tighten around her, and he rubbed her shoulder in a way that she found reassuring.

"Aww," Bree said. "How adorable. Or perhaps I mean pathetic."

"I don't think so," Jake said. "I feel the same way."

"Whatever, it's not your truth," Bree snapped. "Lexie, hurry up."

"Riley," Lexie said. A great idea had just occurred to her. If Jake did think anything had been happening with Riley, this should convince him otherwise.

"Dare," Riley said, smiling crookedly.

"I dare you to kiss Bree," she said.

He looked surprised. So did Bree. So did Jake. A perfect trifecta of startled expressions.

But Riley got up without protesting and sauntered over to their couch. As he leaned over Bree, Jake whispered to Lexie, "Let's get out of here."

She nodded and pulled herself up, tapping Colin on the shoulder.

"Where are you going?" Bree said, shoving Riley away mid-kiss. "Jake, you can't leave your party — it's just started."

"Sorry," Jake said. "I promised my parents I'd be home for a birthday dinner." He lifted his palms up as the others groaned. "What can I do? If I'd known about this, I would have planned differently." He helped Lexie to her feet.

"Well, then Lexie should stay," Bree said with narrowed eyes. "Since she didn't schedule you better."

"She's invited for dinner," Jake said smoothly. "You know . . . because she's my girlfriend."

Bree scowled, and Lexie hid her smile. How did he manage to be so perfect?

"Have fun, guys!" Jake said. "Thanks for the party!"

"Bye," Colin said with a wave. Claire wiggled her fingers at him and he blushed.

"See you tomorrow," Lexie said. Riley half saluted at her. He looked lazy and carefree, as if their intense conversation earlier hadn't happened.

The flustered maid let them out, and as the

front door closed behind them, all three let out relieved sighs. Lexie started laughing.

"What's so funny?" Colin asked.

"We're such freaks," Lexie said. "Normal kids would be psyched about a party, but we can't wait to leave."

"That's 'cause it's a Bree party," Jake said. "I'd rather not be normal than be like those boring people in there. Oh, oops — I forgot my present."

"The expensive leather jacket?" Colin asked.

"Yeah, the one Bree just happened to have lying around," Jake said. "Quick, let's go before she realizes and chases after us with it."

"But it's your birthday," Lexie said. "Don't you want to hang out with everyone?"

"Yes," Jake said, "if by 'everyone' you mean you guys."

"Sadly, I can't," Colin said. "I've, uh, got stuff to do."

They had reached their bikes now. Colin's was hidden in back of the garage, next to a couple of others.

"What stuff?" Lexie said. "What stuff could you possibly have to do in the middle of summer?"

"Just stuff, okay?" Colin said defensively.

"Our hardworking friend Colin," Jake said. "Is it film-related?"

"No," Colin said. "And maybe if I weren't a moron, I wouldn't have to work so hard." He kicked off his bike and pedaled away fast.

Lexie and Jake exchanged puzzled glances.

"Any idea what that was about?" she said.

"Nope."

"He's been acting like that for a week," she said. "I wish he'd tell me what's going on."

"At least you're not ditching me yet," he said. "Want to get ice cream?"

"You don't really have to be home for dinner?"

"Not till nine," he said. "Mom's on call until then." His mother was a nurse at the local hospital. "And I assume you told yours you were going to a party."

Lexie laughed. "She couldn't have been more excited if I'd told her I'd won an Oscar. 'My Lexie! A party!' If I'd given her time to shop, I can't imagine what she would have come up with."

"But then I'd have been suspicious," Jake said.

"Exactly," Lexie said. "So instead you got shlubby T-shirt-and-shorts girlfriend."

"You mean adorable girlfriend," he said with a grin, and pushed off.

Lexie's heart ached as she watched him sail down the block. *Why does he have to be so cute? Why can't this be real? When is it going to end?*

And . . . what's going to happen to me when this is over?

❤ chapter 13

Friday morning arrived.

"Are you ready?" Jake said as Lexie walked down the steps of the porch.

"Ready?" she asked.

"For the pool volleyball finals!" he said. "We're going to win! Rarrr!" He did a cute goofy victory dance, crashed into his bike, and tipped over onto the lawn. She giggled.

"It's like I always say," Jake said from the grass. "Coordination, grace, the ability to stay upright . . . all totally unnecessary in the pool."

"I think our team would have a better chance of winning if I *didn't* play," Lexie said.

"No way," he said, scrambling to his feet. "You have to play. You're essential. You're the heart and soul of the team! Besides, we need five players or Cynthia will disqualify us. You know her; she's a stickler for rules." He grinned and she smacked his shoulder.

"Oh, it's nice to be so vital," Lexie said.

As he pedaled down the driveway, she checked her shoulder bag again. Her black bathing suit, a book to read, sunscreen, and a change of clothes were all there. Why did she have the weird feeling that something was missing?

She must be imagining things. She waved to Colin, who was standing in his window, and took off after Jake.

During tennis, she left her bag, as usual, with the other bags over by the benches under the shelter. She could see it from the courts, but she didn't pay much attention to it, since she was focusing on trying to hit the ball.

It wasn't until the girls went into the changing room at the pool that Lexie opened her bag again.

A sick, nervous feeling shot through her stomach.

Her bathing suit was missing!

She shoved the rest of her things aside, feeling around at the bottom of the bag. Then she sat down on the bench and dumped it out, putting everything back in piece by piece.

It was definitely, definitely gone.

Her breathing seemed to have sped up and she

felt on the verge of panic. Without the bathing suit, she couldn't play, which meant letting down Jake and the team. Sure, it was only a dumb volleyball game, but she would still feel awful about it. And Cynthia was going to be mad. Lexie wondered if you could get detention at summer camp.

"Oh, *dear*," Bree said, and Lexie turned to find her leaning against the nearest mirror. "What on earth's the matter? You look so pale, Lexie, dear."

Sally popped her head out of a stall a few doors down, as if the tone of Bree's voice had aroused her suspicions.

"My bathing suit," Lexie said. "It's gone, but I'm so sure I packed it this morning. . . ." A horrible suspicion hit her. She looked up at Bree, whose fake concerned expression couldn't hide the smirk in her cold blue eyes. "Did — did y —"

"And it's your only one, isn't it?" Bree said sweetly. "That is *so* sad. What *are* you going to do? Your poor boyfriend is so excited about winning this tournament. Oh, *dear*."

"Bree!" Sally said, stomping over. "What did you do?"

"I didn't do anything," Bree said, batting her

eyelashes. "Poor Lexie has lost her bathing suit. And I'm still not speaking to you. Oh, I have a *great* idea, Lexie."

"'Great' meaning 'humiliating,' I'm sure," Sally said, her arms crossed.

"Why don't we check the lost and found?" Bree said, ignoring Sally. She pranced over to a large cardboard box in the corner. "Maybe your bathing suit is here . . . or *maybe* there's *another* one you can wear!" With a flourish, she yanked a bathing suit out of the box and brandished it at Lexie.

It was the most hideous thing Lexie had ever seen. It was a mustard yellow with giant bright pink flowers all over it. There were ruffles at the sleeves, ruffles around the waist, ruffles at the thigh. And it was obviously about three sizes too big for Lexie.

"Perfect!" Bree exclaimed. "I mean, considering you don't have anything else. I guess you either wear this, or you ruin everything for your boyfriend. Hmmmm." She touched one of her long, manicured fingernails to her chin and pretended to look thoughtful, which on Bree looked more like she was trying to pick a new nail color.

"Bree, give her back her bathing suit," Sally snapped. "Give it back right now."

"*I* don't have it," Bree said. "I suppose you could search all over Summerlodge for it. . . . It must be around here somewhere, right?" She smiled, and Lexie felt cold all over.

What was she going to do? She'd never get Bree to give her the suit, and it must be hidden somewhere hard to find. But she did *not* want to wear the yellow flowered monstrosity. If she had any chance of Jake ever wanting to really date her, his seeing her in that would definitely kill it.

Sally looked as worried as Lexie felt. A whistle blew out by the pool.

"Lexie, I have to go out there," Sally said. Her team was up first, playing another team for third place. "You have a little while before your team has to play. You'll think of something, don't worry." Sally started toward the door, then turned and hurried back. She dug into her bag, pulled out her cell phone, and pressed it into Lexie's hand. "In case you need it," she whispered. "And I've changed my mind. Bree is crazy *and* evil." She gave Lexie a quick hug and ran out to the pool.

Bree dropped the yellow bathing suit on the bench next to Lexie. "See you out there," she said smugly, and strolled after Sally, winding her lavender towel around her waist as she went.

Lexie stared down at the phone in her hand.

There was one other option. . . .

She touched the yellow bathing suit and pulled back her hand with a shudder. Had Bree planted it in the lost and found box? Was it just her luck that there really was something so hideous in there? Did that mean someone else had worn it before? It gave her the heebie-jeebies just thinking about wearing it.

She switched on the phone and dialed home.

She was hoping Colin would answer, but instead it was her mom's cheery voice that said, "Hello, hello, Willis residence!"

"Hi, Mom," Lexie said, wincing. "Um — is Colin there?"

"No, he's not, sweetie," Mrs. Willis said. "Is everything okay? Aren't you supposed to be in some activity class right now?"

"Yeah," Lexie said slowly. Where the heck was Colin again, in the middle of the day? If only he were there, she wouldn't have to let her mom know what she'd done with the red bikini. But she had no choice.

With a sigh, Lexie said, "Mom, can you do me a favor?"

"Sure, honey. What is it?"

"I, um," Lexie said, "I forgot my bathing suit."

"And you have the pool volleyball finals today, don't you?" her mom said. Lexie could never predict what her mother would remember and what would just fly out of her brain the minute it went in.

"That's right," Lexie said. "So I need the red bikini. Could you bring it to me?"

"Absolutely," her mom said. She sounded so pleased to be able to help. Lexie felt extra guilty about what was going to happen next. "Where is it?"

"In my room," Lexie said. She could hear her mom's footsteps going up the stairs, and the creak of her hinges as Mrs. Willis went into her room.

"Is it in the closet?" Mrs. Willis asked.

"Um. No," Lexie said. "It's . . . under the bed."

There was a pause. Lexie heard rummaging noises, and then another pause. Finally her mother said, "Lexie, it still has the tags on."

Lexie could picture her mother standing in her bedroom, holding the red bikini with a crestfallen look on her face.

"I know, Mom," Lexie said. "I'm sorry."

"You haven't worn it?"

"I've been wearing the black one," Lexie said, "but I really want to wear that one today."

"Oh, Lexie," her mom said. "You don't have to wear it if you don't like it."

"I do!" Lexie said. "I mean, I need it. As soon as possible. Please, Mom?"

"I'll be right there," her mom said.

Lexie hung up the phone with a sigh of relief. She dreaded the thought of wearing the bikini, but it couldn't be as embarrassing as the mustard-yellow ruffles.

Out by the pool, Bree was lounging on the bleachers next to Riley. She raised her eyebrows at Lexie and made ruffling motions with her hands next to her shoulders.

Lexie scooted up to Cynthia, who was watching the volleyball with the intensity of a bird of prey.

"I forgot my bathing suit," Lexie said. "My mom's bringing it. Can I go meet her?"

Cynthia barked, "Yes! Hurry, but don't run! And don't do it again!" without taking her eyes off the game.

Lexie ran down the path to the parking lot, ignoring Cynthia's instructions. She had been standing there for only a minute when her mother pulled in. Lexie nearly threw herself through the driver's-side window, she was so pleased to see her.

"Thank you, Mom!" she cried. "You saved me, you really did."

"Are you sure you want this?" Mrs. Willis said, holding the bikini out of arm's reach. "We shouldn't cut off the tags if you just want to return it."

"I do want it," Lexie said, leaning in the window. "I do, I promise. Please, please, please."

"All right," her mom said, cutting off the tags with a pair of scissors. "But, Lexie, you should always tell me if I get you something you don't like."

"Impossible," Lexie said, grabbing the bikini and kissing her mom on the cheek. "Thank you! Bye!" She ran back across the parking lot and all the way back to the swimming pool, although she remembered to slow down as she passed Cynthia.

Had that been a surprised look on Bree's face as she went by? Lexie hoped so. She couldn't wait for Bree to realize that her evil plan had been foiled. Unless, of course, the bikini looked as terrible as Lexie was afraid it would.

She jumped into a stall and undressed quickly, carefully putting her bead necklace in the zipper pocket of her bag. The top of the bikini was a halter top, but luckily not the kind you had to tie in the back. Lexie was always afraid those would come undone — or, with her luck, Bree would probably untie it while her back was turned. But this just slid over her neck, and the back was a hook that even Bree couldn't undo without Lexie catching her.

The bottom was simple and fit her perfectly, with a cute decorative knot tied at either hip. And the whole thing was a solid wine red, which, if Lexie had *had* to pick a bikini, was what she would have picked.

The whistle blew out by the pool. The first game must be over. Panic hit Lexie again. Now she had to walk out there like this! She glanced down at her stomach and wondered what kind of girl-hating designer had come up with the idea of bikinis in the first place.

Still better than the mustard-yellow ruffles, she reminded herself.

The whistle blew again. Taking a deep breath, Lexie slipped on her flip-flops and ran out of the stall, grabbing a towel on her way to the pool. She had time only to glance in the mirror as she went by, but she prayed that nobody would even notice her new bathing suit.

No such luck. As she dropped her towel on the bleachers, Lexie could feel Bree glaring at her, as if blunt icicles were jabbing into the back of her neck. She was kicking off her flip-flops when Riley popped up beside her.

"*Dude,*" he said. "You are so *smoking*. I *love* it. Why don't you wear this suit every day?"

"Um," Lexie stammered, "I —"

"Oh, awesome," Sally said, coming up behind her and giving her a giant wet hug. "This is exactly the comeuppance Bree deserves. For you to turn around and look so *amazing*. Holy cow."

"It's nothing," Lexie mumbled.

"Oh, yeah?" Sally said. "Your boyfriend doesn't seem to think it's nothing." She pointed across the pool at Jake, who was staring at Lexie with an unreadable expression on his face. It made Lexie nervous. He looked like he'd never seen her before in his life.

"All right, come on, people!" Cynthia yelled. "Enough chitchat! Into the pool!"

She didn't have to say it twice. Lexie couldn't wait to get the bikini underwater and out of sight.

"I see your sinister plan, you know," Riley said, leaning over the ladder as she scrambled down it. "You're trying to distract me with your hotness so your team will win." He wagged a reprimanding finger at her.

She didn't know what to say to that. Why did he keep flirting with her? He knew about Jake. And it sure seemed like Bree would be interested in dating him, if he'd just turn his charm on her.

Luckily, she didn't have to answer, because Riley slouched off to the other side of the net without waiting for a response. Lexie slid into the water and swam over to Jake, who was holding the volleyball and looking kind of dazed.

"Is everything okay?" she asked, taking her position next to him.

"Uh, yeah," he said. "Totally okay." He shoved his wet hair back and glanced at her sideways before quickly looking away again.

She decided it was maybe not the right time to tell him about Bree and the bathing suit heist. A moment later, Cynthia blew her whistle, and the game began.

After ten days of this, Lexie suspected she was actually getting better. Of course, Riley and Bree were very good, so she didn't expect to win. But Jake seemed to be playing like a possessed person, slamming the ball across the net and spiking it whenever he was close enough. A couple of times he sent the ball her way and she managed to get it over, although Riley was always right there to bounce it back.

When Bree's team reached five points, they switched sides. Riley gave Lexie a wink as they went by, but Bree stuck her nose in the air and wouldn't even look over. She did stop to run her hand across Jake's shoulder, though. "You're doing *so* well, Jakey," she purred. He nodded, looking distracted, and walked away, which made Bree's eyes get even narrower.

Finally the score was 9–9. Jake served, and Riley punched it back. Another girl bounced it up, Jake hit it over, and Bree slapped it into the air like she was batting away a fly. It hung for a moment, suspended, and then fell toward Lexie.

She jumped up to hit it and felt Jake bump her shoulder as he reached forward to knock it up again.

But it wasn't far enough. It was going to fall on their side. Lexie dove forward, her fists connecting under the ball just before it hit the water. She sank below the surface in a spray of bubbles, and when she came back up, her teammates were hooting and hollering and the audience was on their feet, applauding.

She looked around, bewildered, and saw the ball floating on the other side of the net. It had gone over! They'd won!

"We did it!" Jake yelled, splashing over to her. "*You* did it! Woo-hoo! Lexie!" He threw his arms around her and spun her in a circle. She clutched him with a shriek, laughing. She felt giddy. She felt victorious. She felt Jake's warm arms circling her bare waist and it made her feel pretty close to fainting.

"We really won," she started to say as he put her down, but all of a sudden he seemed really close to her, and his eyes were very blue, and then his arms pulled her closer and he pressed his lips to hers and —

He's kissing me!

The universe seemed to spiral into the one perfect, central point where his lips were touching hers, and for a moment that one spot was the only thing she could feel. Then suddenly she felt his hands pressed into her back and her hands on his shoulders, and then she remembered that they were in a pool with fifty people watching them, and then, like something was exploding in her mind, she remembered that this wasn't real, none of it was real, he was just pretending for Bree, and that meant that this, her first kiss, her first real kiss ever, meant nothing at all.

Lexie pulled back so fast that she slipped on the bottom of the pool and stumbled backward in the water. Jake reached for her hand to help her, but she scrambled out of reach, floundering over to the side and pulling herself out as fast as she could.

"Lexie," he said, "wait."

But she had already grabbed her towel and darted into the changing room, where he couldn't follow.

chapter 14

Lexie could hear Sally calling for her through the chaos of everyone changing, but she stayed crouched on a bench in a back stall until Sally gave up and left. She figured if she hid for long enough, everyone else would leave and then she could make her escape without anyone seeing her, anyone staring or pointing.

The whole thing had been a disaster. She would go home and tell her mother she wanted to quit Summerlodge. Or at least she could switch to a new afternoon activity now — like Frisbee, far away from the pool and Jake and Bree and all this torture. Maybe she would go ahead and date Riley. Even if she didn't feel the same way about him that she did about Jake, at least he seemed to really like her. She could have a real relationship instead of a pretend one and get kissed in a way that actually meant something. She hugged her knees to her chest and tried not to think about it.

Finally the changing room went quiet. It seemed like she'd been waiting forever. She was about to stand up when suddenly she heard voices drifting over the thin wall between the stalls.

"Now I get it. It's obvious what's going on." It was Bree. Lexie froze. What was obvious? The fact that she and Jake were only pretending? "I mean," Bree continued, "he clearly feels sorry for her. That's why he's doing this. It's probably a favor for her geek loser brother. But it's just cruel, because he obviously doesn't really like her that way, and she probably thinks he does."

A second voice rumbled something, too low for Lexie to hear.

"Well — *look* at her, for one thing," Bree said. "Guys like Jake don't date girls like that. Come on, she's so awkward and quiet, and she dresses like she's trying to *repel* boys. Plus, did you see how she reacted to that kiss? I told you she was a freak. Like she's too *innocent* to kiss her own boyfriend. Poor Jake. It must be like dating a Care Bear."

Lexie's face was burning. She pulled on her clothes over her bathing suit, trying to hurry out before she heard any more.

"That was pretty lame," agreed the second

voice. A guy? Was there a guy in the girls' changing room? "I expected her to be more mature than that." He chuckled, and Lexie realized he sounded familiar.

"You should have listened to me," Bree purred. "I told you she wasn't your type. *I*, on the other hand . . ."

"You are exactly what guys want," said the male voice. There was a pause. Lexie leaned against the door, wondering if they were gone. She realized that what she was hearing were kissing noises. Who was Bree kissing in the girls' changing room?

"Yes, I am what guys want," Bree said, sounding satisfied. "Jake is going to get sick of the sweet-little-kid act pretty fast. If he doesn't break up with her this weekend, I'll — I'll — I don't know, I'll eat a whole ice-cream sundae or something."

"Why do you care so much if they break up?" the guy's voice said. Lexie strained to hear. Who was it?

"I'm just trying to teach that girl a lesson," Bree said. "A lesson about stealing things from Bree McKennis. And if you really want to know the truth . . ." Her voice went from steely to coquettish. "I was pretty angry that you were more interested in her than in me, too."

Riley!

"That was dumb of me," Riley said, sounding repentant. "I didn't realize what a geek she is. If I were Jake, I'd be like, 'Okay, whatever, loser. I can go kiss some other girl who won't run away when I do it.'"

"Exactly," Bree purred. "Like me."

More kissing noises. Lexie wished she could vanish into thin air and never reappear again.

"So — does this mean we're dating now?" Riley said.

"I told you," Bree said. "You can be my boy-friend . . . *after* I'm through with Jake. I need to show him that nobody says no to Bree, for any reason. Don't worry, it won't be long. He'll break up with Lexie soon and I'll grab him. I'll show him how much better he could have had it, and then I'll dump him so hard he'll never date in this town again." She laughed. "It'll be beautiful."

Lexie clutched the edge of the bench, trying not to make a sound. She wanted to scream and throw volleyballs at Bree's head, but even more than that, she wanted to escape without them knowing she'd overheard.

"Poor little Lexie," Bree said. "She's lost a bathing suit, she's lost a necklace, and she's about to lose a boyfriend. Maybe she'll think twice about taking something of mine in the future, don't you agree?"

"You're so cute when you're evil," Riley said.

Their footsteps were getting farther away, and their voices quieter, but Lexie wasn't listening anymore. Her hand flew to her neck, and then she grabbed her bag and unzipped the pocket.

Her necklace was gone.

She felt tears pushing at the back of her eyes. She had to get home before she cried. She didn't want to cry there, where Bree might find her.

Lexie hurried out of the stall and snuck a look around the door. There was no sign of Riley and Bree. Pressing her fingers to her eyes, she ran out of the changing room and down the path to her bike.

She was already at the Summerlodge entrance when she looked up and saw Jake leaning against the bike rack. It was too late to run; he'd definitely seen her. But she tried anyway, turning to flee back up the path.

"Wait!" he called.

She made it as far as the check-in booth before

he caught up. He grabbed her elbow and pulled her to a stop facing him.

"I have to go home," Lexie said, looking down at her feet. *I have to find a closet I can hide in for the rest of my life. One with cable TV and a never-ending supply of ice cream. That'd be perfect.*

"Lexie, I'm sorry," he said, and the guilt in his voice brought her dangerously close to crying. "I didn't mean to upset you. I — I just —"

"I know," she said, "you just wanted Bree to really believe we were dating. Because why *would* she believe it? You would never date me. I'm weird and shy and I like hanging out with my brother and watching TV and playing with my dogs, and — and I've never dated anyone but you're perfect and gorgeous and funny and smart, so it — it doesn't make sense and of course she's suspicious and of course the only way to prove it is by kissing me, but I —" To her horror, Lexie felt tears spilling down her cheeks. She covered her face with her hands.

"I just wanted our first kiss to be real," she whispered.

"Lexie," he said, and then his hands were on her shoulders and he pulled her into his chest, wrapping his arms around her. She kept her hands pressed to her face, trying not to sob. "Lexie," he said again, his mouth pressed against her hair so she could feel his lips moving. "You have no idea. . . ."

"And she stole my bathing suit," Lexie said, everything spilling out of her with her tears. "And she took the necklace you gave me and I *love* that necklace and — and I heard her talking to Riley about what a geek I am and she's still planning to date you and dump you to teach you a lesson because she figures you'll break up with me now that you know what an immature loser I am but —"

"Wait, wait, slow down," Jake said, taking her shoulders and moving her back so he could see her face. She wiped her eyes and looked down at the ground again. "Did you say she stole your necklace?"

Lexie nodded, her breathing coming less raggedly now.

"That's terrible," Jake said, getting angry. "And you're *not* a geek or a loser — did Riley really agree with her?"

Lexie nodded again. "They were kissing. I guess her plan to snare him finally worked."

"I thought he liked you," Jake said. "But listen,

only a real loser would fall for Bree's act. You know he's a loser now, right? I mean, even though — I thought maybe you liked him."

Lexie looked up and saw his blue-gray eyes only a few inches from hers. He was still holding on to her elbows. *A terrific close-up view of my red, splotchy face,* she thought, ducking her head again.

"No," she said softly. "There's only one person I like." *There. Now he knows.* She took Jake's hands off her elbows and pushed them back toward him. "I don't want to be your pretend girl-friend anymore, Jake."

She turned and ran back to the bikes. He didn't follow her, and she was able to unlock her bike and escape.

chapter 15

There was a knock on the bathroom door. It wasn't Mom's chipper *knock-knock-knock,* her knuckles bouncing rapidly off the wood. And it wasn't Dad's serious, thoughtful *knock-knock,* either. It was more of a *tappity-tap-tap,* don't-mean-to-intrude kind of knock.

"Go away, Colin," Lexie called.

The door creaked open half an inch and a small snout appeared a few inches off the floor.

"I know Thorn isn't opening that door by himself!" Lexie hollered.

The snout nudged the door a bit and soon her pug's entire squashed face was wedged in the gap. Thorn blinked, panted, and snorted, his tongue hanging nearly to the floor.

"Thorn," Lexie said seriously, "I am not in the mood for a face-licking, whatever Colin may have told you."

The pug grinned wider when she said his

name, and as she finished her sentence, he trotted over to where she was lying on the bathroom rug and proceeded to do exactly what he had been told not to. She squealed and pushed him away, which as far as he was concerned was the beginning of the greatest game of all time: try to get to Lexie's face while she shoves you off.

"Colin!" she yelled, covering her face with her arms. Thorn stuck his nose between her arms and her neck and went *slurrrrrrrrp* along her chin. "I'm busy!"

"You don't look busy," her brother said from the doorway. "You look like you're staring at the ceiling."

"I *am* staring at the ceiling," she protested. "It's called moping. Nobody is supposed to lick your face while you're moping. It's very distracting."

"Exactly," he said, perching on the edge of the bathtub. "So what are you moping about?"

Thorn climbed on Lexie's chest, making her go, *"Oof,"* and burrowed into her neck.

"You don't want to know," she said. "And what made you suddenly so Mom-like?"

"You mean nosy?"

"I mean cheerful," Lexie said.

"You tell me and I'll tell you," he said.

She peeked over her arms at him. Thorn seized the opportunity and lunged at her forehead, but she managed to block him in time.

"Are you serious?" she asked. "If I tell you why I'm upset, you'll tell me the big secret you've been hiding all summer?"

"It's not a big secret," he said. "But I guess, okay."

Lexie grabbed Thorn and sat up. He settled down to lick her hands instead.

"Promise not to tell anyone," she said.

"Of course," he said. "Who would I tell?"

"True. But it has to do with Jake."

"Ah," he said, knowingly tapping the side of his nose.

"You *know*?" she said.

"Know that he likes you?" Colin asked. Lexie stared at him.

"No, that *I* like *him*," she said.

"I was starting to guess that, too," he said.

"Colin, you didn't set up this pretend-dating thing on purpose, did you?" Lexie asked.

"No way," Colin said, shaking his head vigorously. "I had no idea then. You guys always acted so normal around each other. I didn't think pretending to date each other would be a big deal. Then you had that date and I was like, '*Ooohhhhhh, I see* how it is.'"

"Really?" Lexie said, blushing. "It was that obvious?"

"That he wants to really date you?" Colin said. "Totally."

"Stop saying that," she said, shoving his knee. "I'm the one who likes him. And now I've told him I can't do it anymore, that I don't want to be his pretend girlfriend, so I'm sure I've wrecked everything. I'm sorry." She looked down at the fluffy yellow bath mat. "It'll probably make things kinda awkward for a while. Oh, why am I such a loser?" She lay back down, letting Thorn flop over on her stomach. "Why couldn't I just pretend and let him kiss me and act like everything was fine?"

"Because you like each other," Colin said. "I don't know why you have to be such morons about it."

"Colin, he doesn't like me that way," Lexie said. "I've had a crush on him forever, but you've seen the girls he's dated. I mean, Amy Sorrento? She's nothing like me. He'll be with somebody new by next week."

"I don't think so," Colin said. "Come on, I want to show you something."

"But I'm *moping*," Lexie objected. He got up and stepped over her, and she followed, rolling Thorn onto the floor. The pug snorted indignantly, shook himself, and trotted after them into Colin's room. As she passed the window, Lexie saw that the afternoon shadows were much longer, she'd been hiding out in the bathroom for at least an hour.

Colin sat down at his computer and plugged the video camera in. Lexie flopped onto his bed, covering her head with a pillow.

"Watch this," Colin said. "The night of your date. Remember, when we all came back here with Sally?"

Lexie peeked out. The camera was on her and Sally. They were rolling balls of dough and getting flour everywhere. They were both laughing, with smudges of white on their faces. The camera panned over to Jake, who was pulling raspberry jam out of the fridge. As he straightened up, he looked back at Lexie and Sally with a smile.

"Hey, girlfriend, get over here," he said,

unscrewing the top of the jam jar. "You've got something on your nose."

"Oh, no, do I?" Lexie said, touching her face and getting even more flour on it.

"Yeah, come here," Jake said with a grin. Lexie came around the counter and stepped closer to him. The Lexie lying on Colin's bed could see the look on that Lexie's face, and she thought, *Man, can't the whole world tell how much in love with him I am?*

Jake leaned forward, studying her face, and then he said, "Yes, yes, there's something . . . right . . . here," and with a studious expression, he reached out and dabbed raspberry jelly on the tip of her nose.

Lexie shrieked and jumped back. "Jake, you dork!"

Jake was cracking up, leaning on the counter for support. The Lexie on camera plunged her hands into his hair and mussed it up, leaving streaks of white flour in it. "That'll teach you," she said, giggling and jumping out of reach again.

"Oh my God," Sally said in the background. "Colin, stop them before they get so sweet our teeth fall out and we can't eat these cookies."

"Don't worry, it's over," Lexie said. "Because *I won*. I'm going to wash my face." She headed out of the kitchen, still laughing.

But the camera stayed on Jake, zooming in as he watched Lexie go.

Lexie in real life sat up.

"You see it, too, right?" Colin said.

"Play it again," Lexie said. He rewound a few seconds and once again Lexie watched Jake watch her.

He had the same look she'd seen on her own face earlier. The same half smile, the same starry eyes. Like he wanted to chase after her and hold her and kiss her and perhaps spend every waking minute of the rest of their lives together.

Wow.

Maybe . . . just maybe . . . Jake was in love with her, too.

chapter 16

"Ha," said Colin. "The camera reveals all truth. I win."

"That doesn't prove anything," Lexie said.

"Proves enough for me," Colin said.

"Then why did he let me run away from him today?" Lexie said. "Why didn't he tell me any of this?"

"Maybe you didn't give him a chance," Colin said.

Lexie pulled the pillow back over her head. This was weird. This was hard to wrap her brain around. She'd spent so long being convinced that Jake couldn't like her and would never like her that it was incomprehensible to think that he really might. It was like suddenly meeting a dolphin with wings. What was she supposed to do now?

"Okay, fine," she said. "So tell me your secret."

Colin actually looked embarrassed. "It's not as good as your secret," he said.

"I don't care," she said. "Spill it."

He picked up a pencil from his desk. "I'm in summer school."

Lexie sat up again. "Summer school? But, Colin, you're so smart."

"Yeah, right," he said. "I failed math last semester."

"No way!" Lexie said. "Why didn't you tell me? How did I not know this?"

"It wasn't exactly something I wanted to talk about," Colin said.

"But I'm your twin!" Lexie said. "You'd think I would have noticed. I feel like such a bad sister."

"It's okay," Colin said. "I asked Mom not to tell you. That's why I'm not at Summerlodge with you."

"Suddenly it all makes sense," Lexie said. "Colin, you could've told me. I still think you're smart. Now I just think there's something wrong with our high-school grading system."

"There is," Colin said with a smile. "They have this crazy notion that we should be taking notes on geometry instead of building model airplanes."

Lexie searched his face. "But you don't seem

upset anymore, like you have been the last couple of weeks."

"Yeah," he said, tugging a sheet of paper out from under the camera. "Look."

It was a math quiz. A bright red 100% was emblazoned at the top.

"Ms. Campbell says I just need to focus, but that I'm very bright," he boasted.

"Well, I could have told you that anytime, silly," Lexie said, batting his head with the quiz. "You didn't have to be a major grouch for two weeks to find that out."

"Sorry I didn't tell you," he said.

"I'm sorry I didn't tell you about Jake," she said.

"That's okay," he said. "If you told me too much of that stuff it would get a bit girly for me."

Lexie glanced behind him at the screen, where the camera was now focused on Sally, who kept looking up at it and laughing.

"Hmm," she said, raising her eyebrows at Colin. "Maybe the camera does reveal all truth."

"Shut up," he said, flicking it off.

"You should ask her out!" Lexie said. "She would totally say yes."

"Yeah, right," he said.

"Would you rather pine over her for three years like I've been doing?" Lexie said.

"You've been pining over Sally Kim?" Colin joked.

She threw his pillow at him. "I think she likes you," she said. "She's much more normal than we thought. It can't hurt to ask."

"Easy for you to say," he muttered.

"I could ask her for you," Lexie teased in a singsong voice.

"Don't you dare!" Colin said, picking up Thorn and shoving him along the bed at his sister. Lexie shrieked as Thorn knocked her over and started covering her face with wet doggy kisses.

"*What* is going on in here?" Mrs. Willis said from the doorway. Alanna poked her nose in, too, wagging her tail.

"Colin threw Thorn at me!" Lexie squealed, wrestling Thorn under her so she could pin him down. The pug snorted and finally lay still, panting happily.

"She totally deserved it," Colin said. "Hey, Mom, look." He held up the quiz.

"Oh!" Mrs. Willis said with a quick glance at Lexie.

"It's okay, I told her," Colin said.

"That's great, honey," the twins' mom said, coming over and taking the quiz from him. "This is terrific."

"Guess I'm not so dumb after all," Colin said.

"Duh," Lexie said.

"Of course you're not dumb," Mrs. Willis said, tousling his hair. He ducked away from her hand but smiled.

"Lexie, how was the volleyball game?" her mom asked, sitting down on the bed beside her.

Lexie's face fell. She'd nearly managed to forget for a moment all the horrible events of the day.

"Oh, you lost?" her mother said sympathetically, patting her knee.

"No, we won," Lexie said. She could tell there were awkward questions coming, so she said quickly, "Thanks for bringing me the bikini. It fits perfectly."

"Really?" Her mom beamed.

"Yeah, you totally saved me. I think I'll take Thorn and Alanna for a walk," Lexie said, scrambling to her feet. She wanted to think about Jake, and she didn't want her mom to ask about him, because she'd have no idea what to say. *We broke up? We were never really dating? I still want to really date him?* It was too complicated. She needed to think.

"All right," Mrs. Willis said. "And by the time you get back, your father should be home, so we can go out to celebrate Colin's quiz grade."

"And Lexie's volleyball win," Colin said loyally.

"Absolutely."

Lexie bundled Thorn off the bed and grabbed her sandals from her room, the dogs trotting excitedly behind her. Downstairs, she dug out their leashes from the basket by the door, hooked them onto their collars, and opened the door to the porch.

Jake was sitting on her front steps.

chapter 17

Lexie would have jumped back inside, but Thorn and Alanna were already galloping over and climbing on Jake with enthusiastic yips.

"Hey, guys," he said to them, tugging on their ears. His cute smile made her want to gallop over there and climb on him herself. He looked up at Lexie. "Going for a walk?"

"Um — yeah," she said. What could she say — no, they weren't? The dogs put the leashes on themselves?

"Can I come?" he said, standing up and sort of awkwardly slouching against the porch railing.

She looked down at the leashes in her hands, blushing. Wouldn't he rather go inside and hang out with Colin?

"I guess, okay," she said. She handed him Alanna's leash, and their fingers brushed as he took it from her.

The dogs scrambled madly down the porch

steps, yanking Lexie and Jake along behind them. They turned left out of the gate and the pugs led the way down the street, snorting and panting and sniffing at everything.

After a moment, Jake said, "Want to hear something funny?"

"Sure," Lexie said.

"After you left, I saw Riley's dad picking him up. Riley said that he wanted to quit tennis and switch to lifeguard training, and his dad started yelling at him that this was what he'd signed up for, that they'd paid for a tennis racket and lessons, and dagnabbit, he was going to stick with the whole program for once and not quit when things got tough like he always did. They were still shouting at each other when they pulled out of the parking lot."

Lexie couldn't hide her smile. "Poor Riley."

"Poor Riley! I'd say he deserves it for what he did to you."

"He didn't really do anything to me," Lexie said. "I wasn't interested in him. I don't care that much about what he said. I know he's one of those guys who let girls like Bree yank them around and tell them what to think."

"An idiot, you mean," Jake said.

Lexie smiled again. "Not like you."

There was a pause, and then they both started to say something at the same time.

"Go ahead," Jake said, but before she could, Thorn lunged at the bushes as Alanna sprinted into the park. The leashes tangled together and around Lexie.

"Thorn, get back here," Lexie said, tugging on him.

"Whoops," Jake said. "Here." He unwound his leash and lifted it over Lexie's head. For a moment, his arms reached around her, and she closed her eyes. *If only* . . .

"Let's set them loose," Jake said. She opened her eyes to find him kneeling next to Alanna. "That'll solve this tangling problem."

"Okay," she said, pulling Thorn closer so she could unclip his leash.

They herded the dogs into the fenced dog run and then shut the gate. Thorn ran to the other end and then back while Alanna sat and looked up at them, panting.

"Can we sit down for a minute?" Jake said. He pointed toward the fountain.

Lexie nodded. She didn't trust her voice enough to speak. She suddenly remembered something . . .

something she'd said two weeks before. Had Jake remembered it, too?

They sat down on a bench where they could still see the dogs. The sun was setting, turning the sky and the clouds pink and gold and purple. The drops of water in the fountain sparkled as they caught the fading light.

Jake took a deep breath. Then he reached into his pocket, pulled out something, and put it into Lexie's hand.

It was a small red origami whale. On the side facing her, he had written, LEXIE . . .

She turned it over. The other side read, WILL YOU BE MY GIRLFRIEND . . . FOR REAL? She looked up in surprise and found Jake's blue-gray eyes only a few inches from hers. He reached over and took her free hand.

"Before you answer," Jake said, "I want to tell you how sorry I am about the last couple of weeks. I didn't know Bree would be so awful to you. I'll get you a new necklace, an even better one, I promise. I didn't know how horrible she could be." He looked down at her hand, running his thumb over her knuckles. "And I didn't know I'd end up falling for you."

Lexie opened her mouth, but he put his fingers

on her lips to stop her. "I'm crazy about you, Lexie Willis," he said. "I think I always have been, but maybe I was too dumb to know it. I want to do all those things for you that I never wanted to do for my other girlfriends, like buy you flowers and call you every night and tell you you're beautiful and stuff."

"But — really?" she said. "Why didn't you say anything sooner?"

"I guess it kinda caught me by surprise," he said. "It took me a while to figure out that I really liked pretending to date you. And when I thought about anybody else dating you — like Riley — it made me feel all weird and mad and crazy inside. Is that dumb?"

Lexie shook her head, remembering how she had felt when he'd started dating Amy.

"And I'm sorry I kissed you at the pool," Jake said, "but I swear it wasn't because Bree was watching. I forgot she was there — I forgot anyone else was there. You have no idea how cute you are in that bikini, Lexie. And I'd been wanting to kiss you for days and I guess . . . I guess I kind of forgot we were only pretending. But I'm sorry if you hated it."

"I didn't hate it," Lexie said, looking down at

his hand holding hers. "That's the problem — I liked it too much, and I thought I wasn't supposed to."

"Then perhaps I'm not sorry," he said. They smiled at each other.

"So," he said, "maybe I've been an idiot up till now, but I kinda thought maybe you were feeling the same way about me."

"Yes," she said.

"Yes, you feel the same way, or yes, I've been an idiot?"

Lexie laughed. "Both," she said. "But I like you like that."

Her heart was beating so fast and so loudly, she was sure he could hear it. Jake touched her face. The look in his eyes said, *I can't believe how much I like you,* and, *I've wanted to do this forever.* Then he leaned forward and kissed her.

And this time, it was absolutely real . . . and absolutely perfect.

Do you ♥ bikinis, too?

Try these two on for size!

From ISLAND SUMMER
by Jeanine Le Ny

"So, I guess you're delivering sandwiches," the guy piped up.

"Huh? Oh. Right. Uh-huh. Maybe you want to order one sometime. I'm sure there's a menu around here somewhere," Nikki replied, fully aware that she was now babbling. She began to search the pile of sandwiches and found a flyer at the bottom. As she tugged at it, a hoagie toppled out of the basket.

"Whoa!" The boy tried to catch it, but it fell to the sidewalk with a splat.

That was when Nikki noticed he was holding a leash, which was attached to a tiny orange Pomeranian, which now had a big yellowish-brown squirt of honey mustard matting the fur on top of its head.

The boy laughed. "Aunt Winnie is not going to be happy about that."

"Oops!" Nikki threw the leaky sandwich back into the bicycle basket, grabbed a pile of napkins, and attempted to wipe off the dog as it yapped and nipped at her fingers. "Sorry!"

"Forget it," the boy said, crouching down and taking the napkins from Nikki. As he did this he smiled and Nikki smiled back, feeling a weird and exciting energy ping back and forth between them. Her stomach suddenly felt as if a hundred butterflies had decided to get together for a game of tag in there.

"Well, I've got to get Button back to my aunt," the boy said, gesturing to the Pomeranian and turning to leave.

"Wait!" Nikki cried a little too loudly. She hoped that it didn't come off as slightly psycho.

The boy turned back and Nikki handed him the menu. "You forgot this," she said. Then, in a bold move, she added, "My name's Nikki, by the way. What's yours?"

"Daniel," he said.

Not knowing what else to do, Nikki casually gazed back into the window of the nail salon, where the women inside seemed to have lost interest, thank *God*. She waited a few seconds to see if Daniel had anything to ask her. Like maybe if he could have her number or something.

Daniel sort of coughed and shoved his hands into the pockets of his enormous camouflage shorts.

Why isn't he asking? Nikki waited a few more seconds. *Maybe he's shy,* she told herself. *Maybe you should just ask HIM for HIS number.*

Why not? *This WAS the twenty-first century, after all.* Okay. She'd go for it. In three . . . two . . . one . . .

"Um, Daniel, I . . . I . . ." *I can't do it!* she thought, chickening out. ". . . I guess I'd better finish my deliveries. . . ." She paused, giving him a chance to talk.

"Oh. Right. No problem," he said, walking backward. "It was really nice meeting you, Nikki." He tripped over Button's leash but recovered nicely. "Heh, heh." He grinned nervously and waved. "Bye, Nikki."

She liked the way he said her name a lot. "Bye." Nikki smiled again and waved as Daniel headed down Main Street with Button. She really wished she'd had the nerve to get his number. He was so adorable and sweet. She wouldn't mind seeing him again. No, she wouldn't mind it at all.

From WHAT'S HOT
by Caitlyn Davis

"I love guys who wear flip-flops."

Holly Bannon watched a guy amble across the large lawn at Mrs. Whittingham's estate, where she and her best friend, Ainslee, were attending a "Welcome to the Club" party. They were both working at the Ridgemont Country Club for the summer, starting the next day.

"I don't know. Isn't he a little short for you?" Holly asked Ainslee, who was nearly five foot nine."

"Crudités?" A caterer holding a tray paused in front of them.

"Sorry?" Holly asked.

"It's an appetizer," Ainslee said. "Take one. Très delicious." She grabbed one from the tray and popped it into her mouth.

"Thanks," Holly told the caterer. She carefully took a small bite of the celery, nibbling the edge. She watched as another guy jogged across the lawn, toward the shuffleboard court on the other side of the in-ground pool.

Shuffleboard, thought Holly. *Who ever even heard of it before tonight?*

"How about him, Ains?" she asked.

"Mmm . . . no." Ainslee shook her head. "Don't like the hat."

"Really?" Holly took another look at him. "You're too picky. I think he's cute. Or he was, but I can't really see him anymore."

"He's all right, but I hate the way he runs. Anyway. We're going to meet so many guys this summer. We don't have to settle for someone who's just sort of okay and wears a baseball cap sideways," Ainslee declared. "My mom always says, 'Never settle.' "

Holly wasn't quite convinced. "Are you sure we're going to meet *that* many guys?" It wasn't as if the Ridgemont Country Club was strictly for high-school guys. *Although that would be cool*, she thought. Except then she couldn't belong to it, which wouldn't be cool at all.

"Are you joking? We are, definitely. I mean, for sure we'll meet more than we did last summer — what were we doing again?" Ainslee tapped the side of her head. "Oh yeah. Now I remember. *Nothing*. For *weeks*."

"But we're going to be too busy working this year to hang out just looking for guys," Holly said.

"Working? Come on. I'll be playing tennis occasionally. You'll be pouring pops. That's only thirty or forty hours a week. That leaves us plenty of time to socialize. And by socialize, I mean flirt."

"There's just one problem. Do we know how to flirt?" Holly asked.

Ainslee laughed. "Not well. But we'll learn."

Holly had to admit that they'd both scored in getting jobs at Ridgemont for the summer. It was the best place to work, because students from all around the area were hired as staff. It was a chance to hang out with a big crowd, and meet someone new, and there were lots of parties over the summer, too. Also, the club's owner, Mrs. Whittingham, believed in letting employees have access to the gym, the golf course, the tennis courts — and most important to Holly, the pool.

Holly pushed Ainslee's arm. "Okay, so. Moving on. Have you thought of a decent way for us to meet those guys yet?"

Ainslee looked around the party. "We're new here, right? So maybe we don't know where everything is. You could go ask them for directions to the bathroom."

"Are you serious?" Holly wasn't about to embarrass herself like that. "Right. Why don't *you*?" she asked.

"No, you."

Holly shook her head. "No."

"Okay, then. Grab a tray. Go over and offer them something to eat," Ainslee suggested. "Then introduce yourself. It'll be natural because you can say you're working for the kitchen this summer, and this is part of the job. Go on. Do it."

"Won't that be kind of obvious?" asked Holly.

"Everything's going to feel obvious to *us*, but it won't be to them. They're guys," Ainslee said.

"They don't notice anything. And remember — we said we were going to be more bold this summer. So. Go."

"Right. Okay. We did say that." Trying to look casual, Holly ambled over to the tent where the caterers had set up.

"Excuse me," she said to a man wearing the standard black-and-white catering outfit. "Would it be okay if I walked around with a tray of something?"

"A tray of something?" He frowned at her. "Why would you want to do that?"

"Well, see, I'm working in the kitchen this summer — the, uh, club café — and I need the practice," Holly said with a smile.

He stared at her as if she had lost her mind. "But . . . the club's café doesn't have waited tables."

Did he have to be such a know-it-all? Holly wondered. "I know, I know, but still. It's customer service, right, so it's good practice. Would it be okay?"

"I suppose. I'll have a seat for ten seconds while you do that. Here, I was just about to bring these out. Shrimp puffs. Make the rounds," he said. "But don't let that group over there take them all." He pointed to the group of guys that Holly planned on making a beeline toward.

"No problem. I'll watch them like a hawk." Holly lifted the tray. "Thanks! This will be great."

"Okay, whatever." The caterer sank onto a folding chair, looking spent.

This is like something out of a movie, Holly thought as she approached the group of guys beside the pool. But it works in the movies, so why not here?

She assumed as casual an expression as possible while she walked up to them. She took a deep breath to compose herself. *Don't say anything stupid,* she told herself. Just make eye contact and smile.

She walked up to the edge of the group and stopped. The guys were joking and laughing about something and didn't notice her at first. *Maybe I should just step away,* she thought as she stared at the back of Extremely Cute Guy's blue T-shirt, which was sort of extremely cute even from the back. Forget this whole idea.

Holly cleared her throat. "Excuse me, would you care for a —"

Extremely Cute Guy quickly turned around.

The shuffleboard stick he had perched on his shoulder came flying straight at Holly's face.

"Ack!" Holly jumped out of the way — and into the pool, feetfirst.

Somehow, because she landed in the shallow end, she managed to hold the tray upright. "Shrimp puff?" she offered as Extremely Cute Guy stared down at her, his friends gathering behind him.

He didn't jump in to rescue her.

He didn't hold out his hand and pull her toward the edge. He didn't apologize for nearly making her lose an eye.

Instead, he just said, "Swim much?" and laughed with his friends. Loudly. At her.

Holly felt like tossing the tray — along with the contents of the pool — back in his face. *Swim much?* What kind of a thing was that to say to a person who nearly drowned — of embarrassment, anyway?

Well, it was one way to meet guys. Maybe not the *best* way, and maybe not the ones you planned on meeting, but still.

To Do List: Read all the Point books!

By Aimee Friedman

❏ **South Beach**
0-439-70678-5

❏ **French Kiss**
0-439-79281-9

❏ **Hollywood Hills**
0-439-79282-7

By Hailey Abbott

❏ **Summer Boys**
0-439-54020-8

❏ **Next Summer: A Summer Boys Novel**
0-439-75540-9

❏ **After Summer: A Summer Boys Novel**
0-439-86367-8

❏ **Last Summer: A Summer Boys Novel**
0-439-86725-8

By Claudia Gabel

❏ **In or Out**
0-439-91853-7

By Nina Malkin

❏ **6X: The Uncensored Confessions**
0-439-72421-X

❏ **6X: Loud, Fast, & Out of Control**
0-439-72422-8

❏ **Orange Is the New Pink**
0-439-89965-6

Point

POINTCKLT